SPECIAL MESSAGE TO READERS

This book is published under the auspices of

THE ULVERSCROFT FOUNDATION

(registered charity No. 264873 UK)

Established in 1972 to provide funds for research, diagnosis and treatment of eye diseases. Examples of contributions made are: —

A new Children's Assessment Unit at Moorfield's Hospital, London.

•

Twin operating theatres at the Western Ophthalmic Hospital, London.

•

A Chair of Ophthalmology at the University of Leicester.

•

The establishment of a Royal Australian College of Ophthalmologists "Fellowship".

You can help further the work of the Foundation by making a donation or leaving a legacy. Every contribution, no matter how small, is received with gratitude. Please write for details to:

**THE ULVERSCROFT FOUNDATION,
The Green, Bradgate Road, Anstey,
Leicester LE7 7FU, England.
Telephone: (0116) 236 4325**

**In Australia write to:
THE ULVERSCROFT FOUNDATION,
c/o The Royal Australian College of
Ophthalmologists,
27, Commonwealth Street, Sydney,
N.S.W. 2010.**

SCOURGE OF THE RIO BRAVO

Blazeville's sheriff was bushwhacked, and Clem Lawson made the mistake of proving a Mexican responsible. Alfredo Garcia and his bandits were rustling the ranches clean, and driving the cattle back into Mexico. The people of Blazeville were scared, and it was agreed that somebody must be found to replace the sheriff. Lawson didn't want the job, but there are responsibilities a man can't refuse, so he was left to take out his resentment on Alfredo Garcia.

JACK GREER

SCOURGE OF THE RIO BRAVO

Complete and Unabridged

LINFORD
Leicester

First published in Great Britain in 1992 by
Robert Hale Limited,
London

First Linford Edition
published July 1995
by arrangement with
Robert Hale Limited,
London

British Library CIP Data

Greer, Jack
    Scourge of the Rio Bravo.—Large print ed.—
Linford western library
    I. Title II. Series
    823.914 [F]

ISBN 0–7089–7750–2

Published by
F. A. Thorpe (Publishing) Ltd.
Anstey, Leicestershire

Set by Words & Graphics Ltd.
Anstey, Leicestershire
Printed and bound in Great Britain by
T. J. Press (Padstow) Ltd., Padstow, Cornwall

This book is printed on acid-free paper

1

CLEM LAWSON looked round quickly from his place at the card table as he heard his name called in a low but insistent manner. There had been something in the voice which had just spoken which had told him that, while he need have no fear for himself in this matter, trouble had come to another and that he was urgently needed to give help or act as a witness. "Deal me out, if you please, Greg," he said to Gregory Sangers, the tinhorn, who was currently shuffling the pack. And then, pushing back his chair and rising, he cast an apologetic glance among the other poker players with whom he had been sitting for the last hour. "Pray excuse me, gentlemen."

A series of nods, which were half curious and half indifferent, came from the men about the table as he swept his money into his pocket and then left the game, striding towards the door at the back of the Hotel San Luis's bar-room, where Max Corgan's long, sunburned face, with its hooded black eyes, sharp nose, neat mouth and pencil-thin moustache, was thrust out at him.

He reached the door. Corgan stepped aside and made space for him to pass through into the service hall beyond. He noticed at once that a door was open in the wall on the left of the corridor and that the shadows of the several people who occupied the room it served were weaving on the hall floor at the end of a shaft of bright sunlight that came slanting in through an unseen window facing south and finally ended its course in the gloom out here. "What's up, Max?" he asked.

"What the devil isn't?" Corgan breathed back at him exasperatedly, features twisted in resentment. "Come on through here. See for yourself."

2

Lawson followed the other towards the open door. Corgan went straight through, but Lawson paused a moment on the threshold. He saw a number of men, all well known to him, clustered around the pool table at the middle of the room. Then he caught his breath as he saw the worn steel brads which were gleaming at him dully from the soles of a pair of boots that clearly belonged to somebody lying there upon the table. He feared the worst. When you saw a man laid out like that, in this part of the world, you could be pretty sure that you had been summoned to take a look at a dead man.

Resuming forward motion, Lawson came to the table. Two men who had been standing almost shoulder to shoulder stepped apart and let him see what was to be seen. Yes, there was a corpse lying there. It was pale, bloody, and the face was in grip of a snarling rictus; not a very nice thing to see. The dead man was Sheriff Bill Bixby, and he had been one of the best too — a friend to the community as well as its servant. "Shot," Lawson observed, when Max Corgan's face turned to him again.

"Straight through the heart," Corgan agreed. "Dead centre. You'll never see a cleaner shot than that."

"Where did it happen, Max? When?"

Corgan grimaced uncertainly. "Two of Lenny Hogan's ostlers found him, Clem — out on the lots. They brought him into the back of the hotel about half an hour ago. Most of the men you see here were called out of the dining room by Ray Collins, the manager. Doc Silk has been examining Bixby. Doc thinks the poor guy has been dead since first thing. Plugged around sunup."

"Hey?" Lawson queried, his brow pinching. "I smell something there that doesn't quite add up. Shot around dawn — presumably on the lots — and not found until this hour? Whatever the time, day or night, a shot fired on the lots would inevitably be heard by almost all the people here in Blazeville. Are you telling me nobody heard the gun go off?"

"Dammit, Clem!" Corgan snorted. "Why do you question everything so closely? I'm *telling* you nothing. I'm only reporting what I've been told or overheard. Some of the men here live out of town — so they can't say much — but those who do live in Blazeville say no shot has been heard about the place in days. While I'm all in favour of folk minding their own business, as a general rule, I can't believe that everybody lost their hearing around dawn this morning."

"It has been discussed then?"

"Of course it's been discussed!" Corgan protested. "It required only a mite of common sense to realize that something was amiss. We aren't all fools, you know, Clem!"

"Max," Lawson said flatly, "I didn't mean to suggest you were. What's the collective opinion of what happened?"

"Shot elsewhere. Brought back here,

perhaps around the breakfast hour, and dumped."

"On the lots?" Lawson mused, considering the nerve which would have been needed to dispose of the body thus, even at an hour of the morning when there wouldn't have been too many townsfolk walking the backways of Blazeville. "Cool."

"Even to making a point, wouldn't you say?"

"El Léon?"

"One of his bunch anyway," Corgan replied. "I'd swear this bears the pawmark of Alfredo Garcia, the self-styled Lion of Mexico. He wants us to know that he knows everything we think and do in this town. It looks to me like Bill Bixby was shadowing one of Alfredo's spies — and the spy got wind of our sheriff. This is the result. Bixby is dead, and the killer is crowing over us with Bill's remains."

"God damn, Garcia!"

"And so say all of us!" Corgan agreed heartily.

6

"But it goes deeper than mockery."

"Sure," Corgan said heavily. "Alfredo likes us to be aware that he's a Yankee supporter. Bill Bixby was *the* sheriff. What better way of showing his contempt for our arrangement to protect our families and property — when our company of patriots goes up to Virginia to join the Confederate army — than by killing the top lawman that we commissioned to look after things in our absence? He's already driven tens of thousands of our cows over the river into Mexico, and this is giving notice that he aims to have the rest. If he can hold us back from service with Robert E. Lee, he'll be a mighty happy man."

"We can't let him do that," Lawson said. "He's had too much success already. Even if we stay and give el Léon a hard time here, he'll still lift cattle elsewhere. He's got pretty well the whole Texas length of the Rio Grande — or Bravo, as he insists on calling it — to pick from, and Mexico

City backing him up for all it's worth. It's their revenge for the war of eighteen thirty-five."

"They're stabbing us Texicans in the back all right," Corgan acknowledged. "What do they think? Do they believe they'll get Texas back if they ruin us and we lose this Civil War? They won't get Texas back whatever happens. If Lincoln runs out the winner of our fight, they'll find him harder to treat with than we ever were."

"The Mexican Empire was too big," Lawson said. "Too big and empty. When Santa Anna sounded the *deguello* at the Alamo, he put the past on trial. History found against the tyranny of Old Spain. We're the future, Max."

"You bet your boots we are!" Corgan amplified grimly. "But that doesn't change much as things stand right now. Alfredo Garcia, *bandido* — because that's what in fact he is — has got us on the rack. If we go up East, he's going to beggar us. And if we stay and protect what's ours, he's going to beggar somebody else who has got the guts to fight our battle. But we can't stay. It's a matter of honour. We owe sword and gun to the Confederacy."

"Has Jason Dwight said what he thinks?" Lawson inquired. "He's our colonel."

"Dwight is the tailor in this town," Corgan reminded dryly. "Not perhaps the best man to ask."

"Our cattle pay for his suits. What if we've nothing to come home to?"

"Oh, he's full of strut, Clem," Corgan sighed, "and far more concerned with why Silas Bolsover, up the river on the Rocking Chair range, won't join our goodly company of Texicans on the ride up to Virginia."

"Bolsover has neither honour nor patriotism," Lawson said dismissively. "He's got a slight limp too."

"Also a mighty pretty wife, eh?" Corgan asked meaningfully.

"I got over that years ago," Lawson said shortly. "The better man didn't win."

"She just happened to love the cripple more."

"Max," Lawson said, slapping Corgan lightly in the middle of the back, "you can be a cruel bastard."

"Is it me, friend, or the truth?" Corgan wondered.

"I try not to think about her," Lawson said. "I haven't clapped eyes on her in a couple of years. As for the rest — agreed. If she were my wife, I wouldn't want to leave her either."

"I guess that's the heart of Jase Dwight's grievance," Corgan said. "Most of us have wives and homes we don't want to leave. Men always suppose that the ones who care most are the ones who show it most." He plunged his hands deep into his trouser-pockets, looking momentarily dejected. "Oh, what the deuce! There's a dead man lying on the table. He was playing pool there last week."

"There's no justice in that, Max."

"The late Bill Bixby has about the same hope of justice as we have of heaven," Corgan said sourly. "Bad day, Clement. I'm going to get slightly drunk in the Cowman's Bar. After that I'll try again. Are you coming, mister?"

"I'll be along in a minute," Lawson responded, far from sure that he was telling the truth, for he had a number of half-formed questions floating around in his mind and wished to gain an answer or two from the more important of the people present who might shortly become his comrades-in-arms; but he hadn't got round to putting his words into shape — or choosing his first recipient for them — when his gaze detected certain blemishes on the dead man's lower attire which he had not noticed before. "Now I wonder — ?" he started up again, looking round for Corgan — since he had something to communicate that could be very important — but his friend had already left the room and passed from sight.

He was tempted to shout after Corgan — who was probably still within earshot — but remembered that this was polite company and that decorum had to be considered; so he shrugged off his impulse and stepped right up to the corpse, bending over it and studying the reddish stains on the washed-out grey of Bixby's canvas trousers. Yes, those oil blotches were shale stains all right and only to be picked up locally in the northeastern corner of his own ranch, the Box L. There were encrustations too, of the same red shale, around the welts and heels of the dead sheriffs boots. Lawson hesitated. He told himself that he could be wrong about this — that he might be jumping to conclusions — but he knew better. The evidence was too plain for that, and it was a fair bet that the lawman had crossed that top right-hand corner of the Box L during the last twenty-four hours — even that he had actually been in that sheltered spot, where those old sheds stood from the hide-and-tallow days, when he had been gunned down.

Come to think of it, those sheds — now around twenty years old and visited only once in a blue moon — would make the ideal hideout for any Mexican who was flitting about the cattlelands to spy out the best herds to rob, and it could well be that Bixby had tracked his quarry to the sheds and then paid the price of trying to creep up on his man by the only practical route present — the narrows between those two buttresses of earth which had admitted the cattle of yesteryear to the green-walled pit which had formed the natural slaughterhouse in which the trapped critters had been pole-axed by the butchers, literally for their skins and candle fat.

The images in Lawson's mind were strong and, as he let them settle, they grew compelling. He knew he must not involve anybody else in this — even his long-time friend, Max Corgan — but he felt that he must go and see whether his theory could be grounded in truth. The ride to that damp place, where the hoof-trampled shale still outcropped amidst ancient blood, would take no more than an hour, and he should be able to do it and get back here to learn any changes of plan that this company might decide on during the afternoon concerning the journey to Virginia. After all, he was still a young man in terms of this day — when age was regarded as the only reliable forerunner of wisdom — and, as had so often been the case already, he knew that he would be excluded from the actual decision-making process here, so the company would lose nothing if he absented himself from the San Luis hotel for a few hours. He jerked his head erect. Yes, he would take himself off; and, yes again, he would visit those mouldy sheds on his land and see if there were any signs around that a Mexican spy had been using them.

In order to obviate any questions that his open departure might encourage, Lawson slipped out of the hotel by its back entrance and then walked round to the front of the building, where his blue roan stallion was tied at the hitching rail. Freeing the beast, he mounted up and rode northwards along Blazeville's sun-cracked and dusty main street, the ammoniac odour of horses strong in his nostrils and the heat of the siesta hour packing in upon him like a smothering blanket.

With its Mexican white walls and red-tiled roofs amidst the cruder Anglo building styles, Blazeville was the average Texas border town and nothing to get excited about, but Lawson had always enjoyed his visits here and knew his life in the district a good one. Indeed, he already felt a faint sense of loss coming on at the thought of travelling into the somewhat alien world of the old states, where the winters could be too cold to imagine and folk had that stiff English way which went back to Plymouth Rock and the days of the Pilgrim Fathers.

He cursed the war as he rode along. There was so much hypocrisy in it.

And not only about causes. Just now he had talked of patriotism and duty — and meant every word of it — but, in his secret heart, he believed that this abruptly enhanced zeal for the Southern cause — into which the more prominent folk of the locality had lately talked themselves — had come too late. This rush to join the flag ought to have occurred way back in '61, when the tides of battle had been flowing strongly in favour of the South. These same men had dithered and postured then, salving their consciences with talk of keeping things level at home to pay for the war. In fact they had been happy to let an apparently victorious army keep bleeding away in its gruelling fights with the numerically superior forces of the Union. If two years ago all the sons of the South had been as ready to get into the fight as he and his Texas friends were now, that Confederate spearhead might well have reached Washington D.C. and the war ended in victory for the Stars and Bars.

But it hadn't happened like that, and the triumph of the North at Gettysburg a month ago had been necessary to spur this sudden wave of ardour to join the regiments in grey. Loyal though he might be, Lawson could not ignore the thought that his friends were starting to sense the growing threat to all they held dear and were getting a touch hysterical about it. This contemplated ride to war, in which he would have his part, was too reminiscent of Bowie, Bonham, Crockett and their like, heading for the Alamo. But in this war, where brother fought brother, there would be no deathless glory. Just final defeat and the eclipse of a dream. But he must put all that out of his mind, pretend to have no doubts, and go right on to the end — first doing what he could here.

Lawson soon put the town about three miles behind him. Now he turned off the trail to his left, angling back a trifle south of west through a desert strip, where cacti abounded and lizards basked on the rocks. Then he came to

17

the northern edge of his Box L range. Here the grass was thin and seldom used as feed. Lifting in his saddle, he looked all around him. There was neither man nor beast to be seen, and the terrain fled into pale, undulating horizons, with a splash of bosque-green where the great river ran and a trace of brown mesa elsewhere. The lonely miles and the blue arch of the sky were the only company in this place.

Quite soon he glimpsed the corner of his property that he sought. It was over to his left and he kept working round towards it, conscious that the grass mounds which enclosed the saucer occupied by the hide-and-tallow sheds seemed a good deal higher and more substantial presence than he remembered. He realized then that he had been nourishing a vague idea, down in his subconscious that, despite all previous experience to the contrary, he might be able to enter the hollow by climbing in over the back of the hillocks; but the formations had outcrops and grassy steeps that discouraged such notions at a glance, and he knew that the portal formed by the two westward-facing buttresses was indeed the only safe way to pass in.

As he approached the natural gate, he bowed over his mount's right shoulder and looked for any sign that the enclosed place had been entered in recent days, but the grass here was particularly thick and springy and retained few traces of any kind. Alert — though not especially uneasy — Lawson rode slowly through the portal and into the shadow-darkened hollow of the dull green area beyond, seeing the ramshackle sheds on his right and feeling the faint chill of the sunken ground. What between crumbling thatch, thick mildew and collapsing beams, the buildings added considerably to the atmosphere of desertion which permeated the place, and Lawson was already fairly sure that he had ridden here on one of those false inspirations that almost every man experienced at some time, when his horse suddenly jibbed a trifle, snuffled out a cautionary sound, and sent puckers running through its hide.

Lawson reined in. Though the stallion was not used to living with much danger, he knew that its instincts could still be relied upon, and he stepped down and eased the Navy Colt out of the holster on his right hip. Leaving the horse now, he began a slow and watchful advance on the decaying hide-and-tallow sheds, moving close enough to the western end of the old-time factory to get a clear view of its nearer corners; but he saw nothing to disturb him further and asked himself whether his own troubled mood had unsettled his horse to the extent that the creature had given out a false alarm. Horses were remarkably sensitive creatures, and Lawson had often felt that the blue stallion behind him could actually read his thoughts. It wasn't so, of course, but the emotional bond between man and beast was too real to be ignored. Yet his own feelings of worry could have played on uncritical brute nature until the creature was deceived as to what he needed of it. But even now he could not quite believe that. There was something here, even if it were only a fox or a coyote lying low.

Still moving very slowly, Lawson started crossing the face of the buildings, pistol held loosely in his right hand but thumb resting firmly on the hammer-togue. The toes of his boots slurred through the grass, the sound adding a ground bass to the lightly swirling music of the breeze, and now he sensed rather than heard a threatening movement not far away.

A definite uneasiness filled him in that moment, and he tightened up all over. He heard his horse blow again, and the noise was louder and more insistent this time. Sure of the warning now, he felt a crawling sensation between his shoulder-blades and up into the base of his neck. Instinct told him that there was a gun pointing at his back. He also knew that there was no second left in which to spin round and locate his target. It all must be done according to his inner awareness.

He threw himself flat, and in the same instant a shot roared.

2

CONSCIOUS as he lay there that the bullet had actually touched his hair, Lawson gave his would-be killer no chance to fire at his flattened shape, but spun over twice — moving rapidly to his left — and then he sat up sharply, his pistol cocked and ready. He saw a chaplet of gunsmoke dissolving, and glimpsed rapid movement behind the black fumes, but no full shape lingered to provide him with a target and he realized that the backshooter had already retreated into the cover of the front corner at the western end of the first shed.

The man had left only the right hand holding his revolver in view. It was no great target, and Lawson had no expectation of hitting it with a snap shot; but he fired all the same;

and, just as the weapon opposite went off for the second time — its bullet flying a yard wide — he heard a shriek from his concealed foe and watched the backshooter's pistol spring out of nerveless fingers as the wrist above the gun blossomed into something that resembled a rose of blood. Now its owner came lurching into the open and collapsed. He lay moaning dreadfully for a second or two, then shut his eyes and passed into what looked like a faint.

Lawson cocked his gun again and closed on the other. He was careful about it, since a cowardly backshooter must be capable of any deception, but the downed man remained inert. Bending quickly, Lawson picked up the other's revolver and thrust it into his waistband. Then he drew back his right foot and kicked his enemy hard, threatening a bullet through the head if any false move should result, but the fellow went on lying as before, his wounded wrist bleeding into the grass, and there could no longer be the smallest doubt that he was genuinely unconscious.

Holstering his Colt, Lawson walked back to his mount, where he unhooked the canteen from his pommel. Returning to the still motionless back shooter, he uncorked the waterbottle and stood over his enemy, now pouring liquid over the other's nape, and presently the man stirred and recovered his senses, emitting a loud groan in the process. "Sit up, you rattlesnake!" Lawson ordered roughly, again putting his toe into the man's body. "You're not that much hurt, by God!"

The shot man clutched at his injured wrist and used his left elbow to jack his torso into a half raised position. He was Mexican all right, but one of the athletic type and no out-and-out greaser. With broad shoulders, narrow hips, long, firm muscles and a wolfish face in which the black eyes glittered intelligently, he could have been pure Spanish stock, but a touch of the

Indian thickened his nose and added that spoiling fraction to the width of his cheekbones. He was a mongrel, but somehow the worse in his evil because he could have been a so much better man. Now he hated Lawson with his eyes, worked up a mouthful of spittle, and spat it out at the Americano's feet.

"Sure, we'll have some of that!" Lawson agreed, reaching downwards with his left hand, seizing the other's shirtfront, and setting him on his feet with an almighty yank. "What's your name?"

The Mexican shook his head and looked blank.

"*Cómo se llama usted?*" Lawson demanded in Spanish, pretty sure that his enemy was deliberately playing ignorant, since few Mexicans who couldn't make themselves understood in English ever crossed the Rio Grande.

"Roderigo Alvarez."

"*Que hace usted acqui?*"

"*Repitalio por favor.*"

"I asked you what you're doing here — and well you know it!." Lawson snarled, switching the waterbottle to his left hand and jerking his revolver again. Then he fired the weapon so close to Alvarez's body that the man's shirt was badly scorched by the muzzle-flash. "Now cut it out, Roderigo! If you want to go on living, speak English — because I have no time for backshooters and there's nobody here who would be able to say how you came by a death wound. Savvy?" The gun went off again, and this time the flesh beneath the shirt was burned a little too. "Savvy?"

"*Si*," Alvarez acknowledged, wincing a trifle and touching the slight hurt to his left side. "*Si, senor.*"

"Now we're getting somewhere," Lawson said in a far more amiable tone of voice. "You're one of el Léon's men, aren't you?"

Alvarez was clearly on the point of denying it, and Lawson thumbed back the hammer of his revolver yet again and deliberately covered the Mexican's heart, only checking the pressure of his finger on the trigger at the very last instant. "*Si.*"

"You killed Sheriff Bixby out here, didn't you?" Lawson demanded. "After that you brought his body into town and dumped it on the lots — didn't you?"

"No, no," Alvarez blurted, horror once more leaping into his face as Lawson's finger resumed tightening on what was already a partially sprung trigger — "*si.*"

"For a moment there," Lawson gritted, "I suspect you could see yourself dangling. We'll hang you all right, and it'll be a terrible way to die — but not less than you deserve."

"But, senor — "

"Oh, you'll get a trial," Lawson promised disdainfully, registering the note of protest in the Mexican's voice. "We'll be strictly fair about it. You'll even get a top-notch lawyer to defend you. But you haven't a hope of beating

28

the charge. Look at the back and shoulders of your shirt! They're covered in blood. You could only have got in that state by carrying Bill Bixby after you'd shot him."

"I haf been forced to confess. Eet ees not in the law, senor, American or Spanish."

"Look at that red clay all over your boots," Lawson snapped. "It was all over Bixby's trousers and footwear too. Just as there's already some on me. How much more proof do you want? Like as not somebody saw you dump the body too. That could well come out now you're caught. I'll be surprised if somebody didn't see you around."

"*Falso!*"

"Sure, a pack of lies," Lawson sighed. "You've nerve enough, Alvarez. I'd put you down for a brazen son-of-dog. But that won't save your neck." He used a little pressure to re-set the hammer of his Colt. "Let's get you back to town. Where's your horse?"

"My arm!" Alvarez complained,

holding up the right limb and still staunching its wounded wrist with his left hand.

"You've got a bandanna," Lawson observed. "Take it off, man, and tie it round the hole. Be damned if I'll take any risks with you!"

"Thees hand I weel nevair use more," Alvarez assured him.

"Says you!" Lawson scoffed. "What's it to be then? Quick about it now — or you'll bleed unchecked all the way back to town!"

Alvarez hastily jerked the neckerchief away from his throat and bound it around his injured wrist. "So — eet ees done," he said sulkily.

"We're going to fetch your horse," Lawson advised him. "If I detect the first sign of any trick on your part, I'll blow a hole clean through you. Understand?"

"*Si.*"

"Go to it."

Alvarez faced about. He walked obediently down the end of the shed adjacent, Lawson just a pace behind him, and turned left at its further corner. Here they came to a strip of grass — which was hidden from the plain beyond by the southern buttress of the portal — and Lawson saw ahead of them a fine black horse that was tied to a post near the open door of a shack which had obviously been cleaned up and made reasonably habitable in recent days. A further indication, at least on the secondary level, that Alvarez's presence in the area was not a new thing. "Bring the horse," Lawson ordered.

The Mexican freed the mount from its tie, the fingers of his one good hand only just adequate to the task; then, while trying to hold together the loose bandage around his wound at the same time, he began leading his mount out to the ground at the front of the shed. Lawson stepped well back to let his prisoner pass, and Alvarez soon reached a position near his captor's stallion. There Lawson stopped him and, walking to his own horse, stepped up, his pistol never wavering off target for an instant. "Mount!" he barked.

Alvarez did so.

"Move out!" Lawson commanded. "Hold your horse down to a walk. We're in no hurry. Unless you're in a hurry to die!"

Alvarez passed no comment. He stirred his horse to just the right amount of movement. Lawson urged the blue stud into the other brute's tracks. They rode out through the portal, and Lawson ordered a right turn. Now they began retracing the route by which he had ridden here from Blazeville, and Alvarez pretended ignorance of this also, but seemed to accept that he was only making a fool of himself when his captor let out a hoot of mocking laughter. After that he led the way to town, and Lawson had to utter no further instructions.

Still travelling at the same walking pace, they entered Blazeville towards the end of the afternoon and the significance of the gun between them evoked little interest among the first onlookers. But, as they moved deeper into town — and passed folk who had a better knowledge of what had occurred during the day — an atmosphere of excitement sprang up. There was a certain amount of hurried talk, and a few shouts were heard; then one or two men went darting on ahead with news of what they had seen. Quite obviously as a result of this, Max Corgan, Jason Dwight, Allan Carstairs of the General Stores, Lem Mace, master of the Double Milliron ranch, Doctor Virgil Silk, and Ray Collins, manager of the hotel, came to the front door and watched as Lawson and his prisoner rode past the San Luis. After that these important men began to follow the pair as they kept their horses trotting in the direction of the sheriff's office.

Another fifty yards brought Lawson's ride to its end. Calling on his captive to halt, he drew rein himself. Then he craned at the men who were following him from the Hotel San Luis, and grinned at Corgan when they caught him up. "Hello, Max."

"I wondered where the devil you'd got to," Corgan said. "You will keep things to yourself."

"Only when I'm not sure about something."

"Where have you been?"

"To the place where that old hide-and-tallow factory stands on my ranch."

"I know the spot," Corgan said. "It stinks of oil."

"If there was anything useless around," Lawson commented wryly, "it would have to be on my land."

"Who's your prisoner?"

"His name is Roderigo Alvarez."

"You caught him yonder?"

Lawson nodded. "Had a hunch. After seeing those red shale stains on Bill Bixby's trousers and boots. You won't pick up marks like that anywhere else locally but on that corner of my ranch."

"I take it that Mexican is responsible for our sheriff's death?"

"He's confessed to being one of el Léon's boys and to murdering Bill Bixby. I reckon he's been spying among our herds for the best spots for Alfredo Garcia to come over the river at and do his stealing."

"That's one fellow better caught," Corgan approved, scowling as Roderigo Alvarez's lupine features came twisting round, full of malevolence. "I'll lay he's had many a tequila at my expense — and a few steaks too. Well, I'm going to have his blood. Hear that, Alvarez?"

"I hear you, *gringo!*" the captive spat.

"Salty villain, isn't he?" Corgan gritted. "How did you persuade him to confess to anything, Clem?"

"Put it down to my natural charm," Lawson responded, tongue in cheek.

"He burn me weeth his pistola!" Alvarez protested. "He keel me if I not spik! I do not do this theeng! Eet weel not stand in court, as you say!"

"Listen to it bray!" Lawson sighed. "I've heard it all before. Please look at the back and shoulders of his shirt. If that isn't the blood of the dead man that he carried a time or two early this morning, I don't know what else it is."

"Lawson, you have the instincts of a born detective!" declared the frock-coated Jason Dwight, a fleshily self-important looking man, with bright, protuberant eyes, a bushy black beard, and a rounded but deeply lined face. "I congratulate you on a fine afternoon's work, sir. Well done!" He looked among his companions. "Won't you add your approval, gentlemen?"

"Well done!" Allan Carstairs echoed amidst the appreciative grunts of the men about him, his great bony head, with its sunken jaw and aquiline beak, nodding vigorously atop the six and a half feet of his beanpole body.

"Thank you, gentlemen," Lawson responded. "But I did it for myself as much as the rest. I've had my losses too."

"Our recent history," Lem Mace of the Double Milliron brand verified. "It's that cow thief, Alfredo Garcia, that we most want here — but this fellow will do for a start. I only wish I could be in town to see him dumped. Jason?"

"I fear not," Dwight responded, leaning hard on the authority that had come to him as a courtesy from the Mexican War of nearly thirty years ago. "The law needs time to run a true course, and you have agreed that I must lead you out tomorrow. There must be no more dilly-dallying. This war needs us urgently, and we can't get to the lines of battle too soon." He signalled a trifle peremptorily to Lawson. "Get that Mexican locked up, Clem, and see to matters here." Now he nodded at the office doorway. "Look, Deputy Sheriff George Hook has come out to assist you."

"Here as ever, Colonel," the paunchy

George Hook acknowledged from the threshold of the sheriff's office, squirting tobacco juice from the rough shaved greyness of his wrinkled mouth. "I've got a nice little room waiting for that long polecat from over the river." He jerked his sixgun, pointing his belly at Alvarez more accurately than the muzzle of his Colt. "Git off that hoss, greaseball — and be mighty careful where you set your feet!"

"*Insulto*, huh?" Alvarez snarled, showing the fat old lawman his teeth as he descended from his mount. "I keek your end, *hombre grueso!*"

"I'm bein' real polite to you, muchacho!" the deputy chewed. "If you want to hear what I can do when I've really got steam up, you keep goin' on how you are!" Suddenly he sprang forward, giving the lie to his age and weight, and let drive with his right boot, neatly burying his toe in the Mexican's rear. "How's that, greaseball? Got in first, didn't I? Well, I'll get in second too — if you don't mind your tongue

38

and get indoors pronto!"

Holding his backside, Alvarez glowered at the lawman. There was little doubt that murder would have been done had the chance appeared; but the prisoner had sense enough to realize that he was up against an old man who would do exactly what he said, so he walked into the law office without further demur. Now Lawson dismounted. He entered the building behind the pair, and was far from sure as to what was expected of him in the time directly ahead. He was also vaguely troubled as the town's dignitaries departed rather suddenly, nidding and nodding among themselves, and headed back in the direction of the Hotel St Luis; for he was pretty sure that there was something new going on among them that concerned him a little too closely. You couldn't trust anybody; and your best friends least of all.

He saw George Hook grinning at him from the other side of the room. The deputy had just taken down a ring of keys from a nail that jutted out of the wall behind the incumbent's battered old knee-hole desk. "You ever figure you'd have to come into this rat-hole, Mr Lawson?" he inquired, sounding vaguely pleased about the rancher's presence.

"Guess not, George," Lawson responded good-naturedly. "Can't tell you how sorry I am about your boss. I liked Bill Bixby."

"Most everybody did," Hook agreed seriously. "I'm still not quite straight. Was it this skunk, sir?"

"It was him all right, George," Lawson answered.

"Pity lynchin' has gone out of fashion, sir."

"Now, George!" Lawson chided. "Was that a slip of the tongue?"

"Fellow can think aloud."

"Do it myself sometimes," Lawson admitted. "Anyhow, let's get this man locked up."

"Through here you!" Hook ordered, jerking a thumb at the prisoner and then opening a door in the rear wall of the office and providing a gloomy view of the lock-up passage beyond. "You keep him covered good, Mr Lawson. I have to deal with these keys."

"Don't worry yourself, George," Lawson said as they entered the jailhouse. "I've had him covered for the last hour or so, and he's been a good boy up to now."

"Sir, I'd be a good boy around you," the deputy confided, unlocking the cell at the end of the row on their left. "You're a gentleman bred and born — but I always have said you're the hardest man in town. Maybe in this part of Texas. Used to tell Bill so. I sure don't envy them blue-bellies. Reckon you'll go through them with fire and sword."

"Don't overdo it, George," Lawson said soberly. "I'm just another man. A bullet in the right place would do the same for me as it'd do for you — and the Mexican here."

"Only it'd be a pity about you and

me," the deputy opined, spitting with accuracy into the prisoner's tin pail at the back of the cell as he jerked his thumb again. "In there, greaseball! Oh, to hell with your poor wrist! Don't you let me hear a word out of you I don't want to hear. At that, I ain't leavin' you a lot o' scope, my bucko, but that's how it is. I'm gettin' old, y'know, and I like a quiet life. I'm sore about Bill Bixby too, and when I'm sore" — his toe lashed out at Alvarez's posterior again — "I'm real sore!"

"Lock him in," Lawson commanded, putting on an expression calculated to deter as the Mexican rounded on the deputy with his left fist raised.

Hook obeyed and, with the bars now separating them, held up his keys and jingled them in the prisoner's face. "Senor, you're done for!" he declared. "All you've got to look forward to is the moment that rope snaps your neck! And not even to that, I reckon — 'cos Old Nick will sure be waiting to catch you and take you gallopin' off to hell! *Comprender*?"

Alvarez made a lewd gesture that would have meant the same thing anywhere.

"He's got the idea," Hook said inconsequentially, as they walked back into the office and he left the door of the jailhouse standing slightly ajar behind them. "I'll do my job by him, sir, but peace o' mind I ain't going to let him have."

"Well, you're the man in charge here now, George," Lawson observed. "It's an ill wind, as they say. I guess Bill's death means promotion for you."

"Not a chance, Mr Lawson!" Hook said dismissively. "I'm too old, too fat, and too dumb."

"Dumb?"

"As in stupid, sir."

"I know what you mean," Lawson grinned. "But — dumb?"

"I'm literate."

"Illiterate?"

"That's the one," George Hook

43

agreed, perhaps secretly proud of himself — if only on account of the word's length.

"That's a shame."

"Bill did all the writing."

"You do the running?" Lawson asked, smiling sympathetically.

"I have my uses, sir."

"Of course you do!" Lawson acknowledged. "So let's sort ourselves out. What's the normal procedure when you lock a man up, George? I imagine some writing has to be done."

"Customary," Hook said, chin jerking up and down.

"What has to be written?" Lawson inquired. "What form does it take?"

"A report for the County Sheriff's Office," Hook explained, his mouth becoming more sluggishly elastic as a corner of his eye sought the spittoon. "Has to be done right — 'cos a dupplekate is passed on to the County Prosecutor and them as may be asked to defend the mallyfactor."

"I see," Lawson said, grinning to

44

himself under a raised eyebrow. "Well, I can hardly leave you with that responsibility, can I? Tell you what, George, you can fetch Doc Silk to have a look at the prisoner's wound, and I'll sit down at that desk and write a report for the County Sheriff on how and why Roderigo Alvarez was arrested." He fixed the deputy with a level stare. "How does that sound to you, George? Fair division of labour?"

"Jim-dandy, sir," the deputy replied. "Sounds real jim-dandy!"

"Okay," Lawson said, moving to the desk, "I'll get right down to it. And before you go — Where's the writing paper kept?"

There was no answer. Lawson glanced quickly at Hook. He did not believe the other could possibly lack the answer to what he had asked. Then he saw that the older man was now standing rigidly and listening at the jailhouse, neck corded with the intensity of his concentration. "What's up?" Lawson demanded tensely.

"I'll swear he's talkin' to — " Hook hissed in reply, breaking off as he again moved with surprising speed and threw the cell block door open before plunging down the passage beyond.

Lawson went after the man, fearing that a rescue attempt might already be taking place.

3

GUN lifted, Lawson checked abruptly as he came to a full view of Alvarez's cell. The Mexican, hands on the bars of the grille which admitted light to his place of imprisonment, had lifted himself up the wall and, with the toes of his boots dug into the brickwork to hold him in place, appeared to be listening to what somebody who was hanging in a similar position on the other side of the bars was saying to him.

Lawson faced about. Racing out of the jailhouse, he made for the open front door of the law office and the street. Passing outside, he turned left and headed for the alley at the end of the building in that direction. Coming to the narrow way, he entered it and pounded down its length — almost literally exploding into the yard at the rear of the jailhouse and screwing his head towards the grille at which the illegal conversation had been taking place — but the intruder had already jumped down from the cell window and passed round the corner of the sheds on the right that formed the border of the lots adjacent, as his racing footfalls betrayed.

Putting in another spurt, Lawson made after the sounds. He reached the corner of the sheds in two seconds or less; but even so, on making his own right turn, he perceived that his quarry was remarkably fleet of foot and had already gained a good lead on him. The other was whisking away through the oakbrush and domestic debris with which the eastern border of the town was cluttered at a rate that he could not even match over open going. Feeling baffled by this, but still pursuing as fast as he could, Lawson did all in his power to gain a single clear look at the unknown person ahead; but, though he dodged in this direction or angled his gaze in that, the one unobstructed glimpse he sought eluded him, and his quarry remained unidentified by him as they neared Blazeville's southern limits.

Lawson both feared and rather expected what happened next. For suddenly the fugitive swung away to the right and entered an alley which connected the back ways of the main with the street itself. Sixty yards behind the other — and with his lungs already straining and his heart thudding against his breastbone — Lawson instinctively did the only thing he could to stay in the chase and turned into a parallel alley, hoping that he might still reach the street through it in time to gain a sure glimpse of his man before the other entered a new stage of his flight.

Once again Lawson hurled himself between walls, striving to keep more or less abreast of the fugitive moving in the same direction up street of him. The shadows were black about him, and the underfoot littered and uneven. He tripped on a piece of timber just short of the street. Reeling and staggering, he banged first one shoulder and then the other against the brickwork that confined him on either side, fighting to keep his balance; but, though he managed this, arrived on the beaten way a full second later than he expected and was in time to receive only a fleeting impression of a figure passing into an alley just about opposite that from which the fugitive must have emerged on what was still Lawson's own side of the road.

Now Lawson attempted to repeat the parallel movement that he had just used, but there was no passage conveniently placed to meet his need on this occasion and he was forced — as he picked up his stride again — to slant off to his left and cover ground until he could follow his quarry exactly, entering the alley which the other had used well after the man had cleared it. A few moments later he breasted out on the land to the west of Blazeville and came to the final frustration of seeing the fugitive spring onto a horse standing in a cluster of cottonwoods about a hundred yards away and go bursting down a tunnel of green towards a vignette of slightly undulating country beyond.

Coming to a stop, Lawson bent forward and gasped for breath. He peered narrowly at the ever-decreasing shape of the escaping horseman. It remained impossible to identify the other, but he did get a glimpse of a bottle green shirt and the woven disc of a sombrero hanging down the fugitive's back. He also had the impression that the receding horse was what was known as an Indian Red — a not too common shade of mount — and it seemed to him that this combination of colours and shapes did jolt his memory a little. A name came at once to mind — a Mexican name — and he thought it might fit in with what had just happened; but he could not be sure. And you had to be sure before you could accuse. Now the rider dropped beneath the land and was lost to sight. Well, that was that; there was no point in dwelling on any of it further for the minute. If only he had had a horse available to give immediate chase across the land!

Lawson straightened up, his breathlessness much reduced. It occurred to him that he was still holding his Colt in the almost bruisingly tight grip of his right hand, and he thrust the weapon away. After that he turned and walked back through the alley to the main street. Here he bore left and made for the law office. He saw Deputy Sheriff George Hook standing outside the building and gazing towards him. "Have you nothing better to do?" he asked shortly, as he approached the man, though his resentment of the deputy's apparent idleness reduced abruptly as he saw that Hook's hands were covered with blood. "Have you hurt yourself?"

"Ain't my blood," Hook answered

a trifle sullenly. "It's that greaseball's. Alvarez has gone and done somethin' real bad to that wrist of his. That's what he gets for hangin' about monkey-fashion."

"Oh?"

"He blundered off the wall," Hook went on. "I guess I scared him some. That wound of his started lettin' blood like a fountain. I could see bits o' white bone coming outa the hole. I've got that snake all muffled up in towels."

"That's all very well," Lawson said. "It's Doc Silk we need here. I did tell you to go and fetch him. It needs few brains to work out he's most likely in the San Luis with the other gentry right now."

"You going to look after the prisoner?"

"I hope to goodness he's locked up, George!"

"He's locked up." The ageing deputy scowled. "God-dammit, Mr Lawson! Keepin' guys under lock-and-key is my business!"

"Quite so."

"Who was that you chased down the back of town?"

"God knows!" Lawson snorted. "I didn't get close enough to see."

"Bill Bixby would have done better than that."

"Very likely," Lawson conceded. "But I am *not* the sheriff, George. Nor am I ever likely to be."

"You can say that again, sir," Hook responded bluntly.

"Very well," Lawson said resignedly. "You get back to your prisoner, George. As you say, that's your job. I'll go and find Doc Silk for myself."

"If that's how you want it," the deputy acknowledged grumpily, facing round and stamping back into the law office. "Damn a fellow who can't make up his mind."

Lawson walked on. He wasn't very proud of himself. Underneath all the nicely picked words, he had been taking it out on George Hook for his own poor performance. What had he to resent in himself anyway? He had done all right today. If he wasn't the fastest runner in the district, he was probably only one of a thousand who couldn't have kept up with the man who had been so quick to contact the imprisoned Alvarez. Yes, the speed with which that had been done pointed still more firmly in the direction of the man that he, Lawson, now suspected in his own mind. It figured the guy had actually been riding towards the hide-and-tallow sheds — perhaps on a liaison mission of some kind — when he had spotted across the land that Alvarez had been taken prisoner. If the man, as Lawson thought, had been coming from the direction of Silas Bolsover's 'Rocking Chair' ranch, where he was employed, he would have been advancing from the southwest of the sheds and most likely hidden from any observer to the east of him by the glare of the sun. The deductions were not improbable ones, and they made a lot of sense; but there was still no proof of anything. Nor would the explanation of it be likely to help mollify the perhaps justly indignant George Hook. Oh, to blazes with it! He knew where he had really gone wrong. He had been too ready to involve himself in all this. He had only himself to blame for his present troubles.

Entering the Hotel San Luis, Lawson walked straight through to the Cowman's Bar. He saw all his friends there — Doctor Virgil Silk included — and they were seated about the big round table that graced the centre of the room. He saw, too, that bluff Sam Wilberforce, the Mayor of Blazeville — who would not be travelling to war with the volunteers — had now joined the men with whom he had had earlier contact in the pool room; and it was Wilberforce, ruddy of face and booming, who called: "Come here, young Clement! I want you, boy! We've been discussing you — favourably! Yes, very favourably!"

"Well, I thank you for that, Mr Mayor," Lawson responded. "But, if you'll excuse me a moment, it's the doctor that I'm here to see."

"What's wrong, Clem?" Silk asked amiably, living up to his name in the sleek tailoring of his coat and trousers, the tasteful pattern of his waistcoat, and the smooth perfection of both his shave and pomade. "You're looking hot and bothered, my boy!"

Lawson nodded dismissively, a little disconcerted by these sudden and somewhat unusual references to his relative youth. "It's that Mexican, Alvarez, I brought in a while ago," he explained. "I wounded him, and ought to have asked you to examine the wound earlier. It seems he's hurt himself further and is now bleeding very badly. There could be danger. Will you go along to the jailhouse, please, and see what you can do for him?"

"Why, surely," the doctor answered, rising from the table. "Who's with the man now?"

"George Hook."

The doctor cleared his throat

expressively. "I'll leave this instant. Excuse me all!"

"Yes, run along then, doctor," Sam Wilberforce encouraged.

Virgil Silk withdrew.

Then the mayor looked at Lawson again and said: "Clem, we've lately held a brief but purposeful pow-wow in here. Jase Dwight was mightily impressed by the arrest you made, and he's been speaking eloquently about it. Though more especially about you, as a man, and what appear to be your particular talents." He smiled, taking out his silver snuffbox and tapping on its engraved lid. "Are you with me?"

"As far as you've gone, sir," Lawson answered, beginning to fear what the other could be coming to. "I simply use my very average powers of observation more than most people, and I've a bit more nerve than some."

"You're too modest, Clem," the mayor assured him. "You not only see what's there, but can assess what ought to be done. You know how and when to act. These gifts may sound commonplace, but they aren't so ordinary." Opening the silver box, he helped himself to a pinch of snuff, drawing the brown powder deep into his nostrils. "How much do you want to go to war?"

"As much as any man here," Lawson answered.

"Nicely put," the mayor approved, though maybe a touch cynically, as he wiped his nose with a linen handkerchief "Can't make too much of that, can we? It can either be a patriotic utterance — or a neat little piece of sophistry, eh?"

"Since you're not going anyway, Mr Mayor — " Lawson reminded, just too innocently.

"You could be making my point, Clem," Wilberforce said rather cunningly. "I shan't be going north because somebody has to stay. Answering the call to battle can be a self-indulgence."

"I wouldn't presume to judge,"

Lawson admitted. "Life has to go on behind the war."

"Son."

"Sir?"

"The men gathered here want you to stay behind."

"But that's ridiculous!" Lawson protested.

"I know, I know," the mayor soothed. "You're the youngest, fittest, and best with pistol and sabre. All perfectly true. Yet there are still thousands of men in Texas able to fight the Yankees, while there are only a handful who can do those things necessary to the future of all. These men wish to leave the law behind them, and to place its enforcement in the most able hands available. By general agreement, those hands are yours."

"Merciful heavens!" Lawson ejaculated, feeling about as depressed as he had ever been — particularly in view of his dismissal of the very thought in George Hook's company not so long ago. "All this on the basis of catching

a killer. Luck played its part in that!
Now you want me to take the late Bill
Bixby's place as sheriff."

"Not as such," Wilberforce said
carefully. "You would have a much
wider authority. Your title would be
the District Marshal. You'd have the
right to call on every man in the district
to fight wrong-doing. That's the limit
of the power that we can bestow. The
County takes over beyond that."

"Sheriff — marshal. What's in a
name? It's the same job." Lawson
scowled about him rebelliously. "I
don't want it!"

"We can't force it on you," the
mayor sighed. "This is an appeal to
your public spirit. Neither more nor
less, Clem."

"I'm a rancher."

"You've made arrangements to go
to war, haven't you?" Wilberforce
reminded.

"Hugh Brakes, my foreman, will be
taking over as the manager of the
Box L in my absence."

"There you are," the mayor pressed. "Brakes can still manage while you're marshalling. You'll have the added advantage of being able to keep a watch on your affairs until things return to normal."

"If they ever do," Lawson muttered. "No. There must be somebody else, Mr Mayor."

"George Hook?"

"He's a good man," Lawson declared, "but — "

"Yes, there's a 'but'," Wilberforce agreed. "There are lots of 'buts', Clem. I fear we could attach a 'but' to just about every man that we might name here."

"I could hang a string of 'buts' around my own neck," Lawson observed sourly, "if it comes to that. But — there it goes again — I fear you gentlemen are in no mood to listen."

"We can't force it on you," the mayor repeated. "No need to get your dander up. Why don't you go home and think about it?"

"You've got until eight o'clock tomorrow morning," Max Corgan put in ironically from the further side of the table.

"Oh, yes!" Lawson snorted. "Depend on you!"

"You've got that a little wrong, my man," Corgan said pleasantly enough. "We're depending on you. This has been properly talked out. That's from the guy who was planning to ride at your elbow."

"So even you think — "

Corgan raised a staying hand. "I'm not saying another word, Clem. It's all up to you."

"You sure know how to twist a man's arm!" Lawson accused. "All right, Mr Mayor. I'll go home and have a think about it."

"We'll look for your decision in the morning," Wilberforce said. "If you ride into town packed and ready for the trail, we'll know the worst and say no more about it."

"I expect that's how it will be,"

Lawson said, nodding farewell to the men seated about the round table. After that he left the bar-room and strode back to the street with the same directness which had characterised his earlier entry of the hotel.

The heat of the day was still considerable, and he paused to finger a drop of perspiration away from his brow. Then he looked around him for his horse, still suffering a certain confusion of mind — perhaps resenting that he had been put under pressure by people who knew him to be a man of conscience — and it was a moment or two before he realized that the mount must still be standing outside the sheriff's office.

Catching a toe in a broken section of the boardwalk — and cursing on that account — Lawson headed southwards. He arrived at the door of the law building about half a minute later. His big blue horse was still standing much as he had left it. Drawing it away from the hitching rail, he put a hand on his pommel and paused, wondering if he ought to walk through to the jailhouse and find out how Doc Silk was getting on. Courtesy almost demanded the visit, but Lawson discovered that he lacked the patience just then to watch the physician treating a man who would most probably be hanged at some time during the next few weeks. It really did strike him as a waste of the doctor's skill and energies.

Mounting up, Lawson set the stallion trotting southwards. His mind remained in a minor turmoil, and the horse had carried him clear of Blazeville before he was aware of it. He kept telling himself that he was a free man and had no decision to make, yet he knew in his heart that he had one all the same. When a man became part of a community, he owed obligations to that community. He had been requested by his fellows to provide them with an important service. He could not turn his back on the whole affair and pretend that nothing had happened. Nobody in

Blazeville had ever let him down when it mattered, and he could recall several outright favours received. He was in that sense owing. Yet still he felt that he could do more good elsewhere. Surely somebody at least as smart as he could be found to keep the law around here. These were parlous days. He was being denied this chance to break away from — his responsibilities? Was that it? He felt jolted all through. Had he been deceiving himself? Was that what Sam Wilberforce had been driving at? Could he have been behaving like a spoiled child who had been trying to show that his play was more important than the work which must be done? The human mind could indeed prove an ugly stamping ground for the devils of self-will. It looked like he would have to rearrange his thoughts on this matter, and then think it through again — which was still more sobering, since he had not seriously intended to consider any change at all.

He yawned cavernously. All of a

sudden he was very tired. Worry took more out of a man than hard work ever could. He viewed the trail before him. The ride to his home on the southern border of his ranch was one of only three miles. Nothing at all; and normally he regarded it as such. But today those three miles seemed to stretch interminably.

Perhaps he ought to take himself off the trail and have a rest — do his thinking about as far away from people as he could get locally; but then he saw an American cream mare standing beside the beaten way and his interest quickened — causing him to look down the shallow slope of grass beyond and through the line of trees at its foot, to where the surface of a small lake glistened and shifted as the rising breeze passed through the shadows of the westering sun.

Lawson drew rein. Lifting a little in his stirrups, he peered more closely at the lake's nearer bank. He saw a tall, brown-haired woman standing there.

She was clad in tan riding attire, and a black plains hat hung down behind her shoulders. Her head was set at what for him was a familiar angle, and she appeared to be gazing at her own reflection in the depths. Tina Bolsover? The woman he had once regarded as his Tina? It was a long time since he had last seen her in this part of the district — or any other part of it for that matter; and, while a man didn't go accosting married women — regardless of how well he might once have known them — he felt reckless enough just now to bend the rule a little and join Tina Bolsover below. If that didn't suit, he knew Tina would tell him soon enough. Forthright that girl had ever been!

Smiling wryly to himself, he dismounted. He left his horse at the opposite side of the trail to the cream mare. After that he moved onto the slope adjacent at a slow run, stumbling down the last of it into the trees, and then striding on through to where the woman stood beside the lake. "Hello, Tina," he said, as the flawless oval of her slightly startled face suddenly craned at him. "Why so pensive?"

"Oh, it's you, Clem," she said, as if there hadn't been a year or two between. "You're looking a little jaded yourself."

"Becomes me," he teased. "The ladies tell me so."

"And you'd listen," she agreed, a knowing smile just touching her soft brown eyes and delicately curved lips. "I hear you and the rest of them are soon off to the wars."

"Tomorrow, so the rumour goes," he answered. "You didn't come here to say goodbye?"

"I hoped if I rode over this way I might run into you, yes," she said with her usual disconcerting frankness. "You might get killed. I'd like to be able to look back and say that I wished the hero farewell."

"Be able to say, eh?"

"Not in the parlour."

Lawson chuckled. "So the old man can be jealous?"

"Silas can be a lot of things," Tina replied, the fun draining out of her with an abruptness which seemed an unexpected shock to her and left her looking at him with an air of slightly confused guilt.

"What's wrong?"

She hesitated, twisting hard at the dark leather plaiting of the silver-mounted quirt that she was holding between her hands. "Nothing — nothing."

"Happy?"

"He's been a good husband, Clem."

Lawson eyed her narrowly. A simple 'yes' would have done, and been far more appropriate.

"Can I help, Tina?"

"With what?" she asked, smiling again.

But he knew that she had not yet fully recovered herself — or managed to get out what she had really wanted to say. He said nothing, prompting her with his eyes and waiting.

"There's — there's so much going on, Clem."

"Wasn't there always?" he queried.

"I suppose so."

"Maybe I should have asked — like what?"

"No, you shouldn't."

"Tina, you know I'll always be — " he began, checking himself sharply. "Tina, you know I'm your friend for life. There's no past or future for that. It simply is."

"For life," she murmured, as if there were some kind of sentence involved; and adding drearily: "Oh, Clem!" Then, after a long moment, she hurried out: "Well, I hoped to be able to bid you farewell. I have done so. Adios, Mr Lawson."

"Ditto, Mrs Bolsover," he responded, making no effort to hold her and watching with a frown that was both baffled and worried as she hurried away from him through the trees and thence up the slope towards the trail.

71

There was something wrong there. Tina had been suppressing the very truth of her own nature. What was it she had wanted to tell him — yet dared not?

4

LAWSON arrived home about half an hour later. He was frankly sore of heart and mind. Nor did it do his spirits any good when he came upon his foreman, Hugh Brakes, seated in the parlour and drinking tea with Mrs Dupont, his housekeeper. The pair looked real pally, as if the manager designate had already taken up his position and been accepted by the chatelaine. "What cheer, you two?" he greeted, as he pushed in from the hall. "Can you squeeze a cup out of that pot for me, Sarah?"

"Certainly, Mr Lawson," the plump and ageing lady responded, rising to pour for him as he cut himself a slice of farm cake. "Have your friends made up their minds about the date yet?"

"Tomorrow, Sarah," Lawson answered. "They're leaving Blazeville at eight o'clock tomorrow morning."

"Well, you've got your warbag packed and ready, sir."

Lawson nodded curtly. "What are you in here for, Hugh?"

"Looking for you, boss," the rangy, fair complexioned Brakes replied. "I was hoping I'd find you here."

"You too often haven't of late," Lawson admitted. "So what is it?"

"It comes down to moving tools really," Brakes explained. "There's not too much on right now. We're at the start of that slow time we always get before the fall round-up. I've got guys who might as well dig as ride around doing nothing. I'd like to cut into that stream which runs off the West Hills and divert some of its water for our use. We have discussed it — "

"Tentatively," Lawson acknowledged. "It must be done at a spot where the flow is still well on our land."

"Goes without saying, boss. I don't aim to involve you in ructions."

"You hadn't better," Lawson said

flatly. "Will what you plan substantially rob the main stream?"

"Substantially, no," Brakes said a little uncertainly. "But it will lower the water level a mite on the 'Rocking Chair' range."

"I don't know about this," Lawson sighed, seating himself in a chair beside the window and twisting round to look upon the river country to the south of his home. "Damned if I want to take any risk of antagonising Silas Bolsover. Dry summers are the snag."

"Your cows on the west graze do all the suffering now," Brakes reminded. "It's a beef-stripping climb up to that stream when the waterholes below run dry."

"There's nothing spring-fed," Lawson allowed. "It's all run-off water and dependent on the sky. I can't see that Bolsover's herds would suffer, so I do feel that I have the right — "

"So do it, boss," Brakes urged. "It's not your fault you won't be around to have it out with Bolsover. Anyhow, I can talk up to 'Clubfoot' for you. He don't scare me any."

"It's not a question of that," Lawson snapped. "I may still be around yet anyhow. You'd better understand me correctly, Hugh. This isn't a matter of standing up to somebody, or arguing a dubious matter of principle if it comes to that. This could turn out a simple matter of be done by as you did. If you ask other folk to do what's seen to be right, you've got to do what's seen to be right yourself."

"I don't get this," Brakes said. "You said you may still be around."

"I've been offered a job."

"You've what?"

"Well, sort of had it wished on me then. It won't make any difference to you and running this place. I'll still be elsewhere ninety-nine percent of the time."

"What is this job, boss?"

"District Marshal," Lawson replied. "It's a new title Wilberforce and the rest have thought up. There must have been some kind of blessing from the Judiciary. The sheriff — Bill Bixby — was murdered today. I caught the killer. This came out of that."

Brakes nodded thoughtfully. "I'm sorry about Bixby."

"Yes."

"But you've got a choice?"

"I've given myself one."

"I wouldn't have thought — "

"That I had any?"

"Not as the bigwigs asked," Brakes said frankly. "I sort of figured their wish for a command, boss. Somebody has got to keep the law. Even if the god-damned Yankees come, that'll stay true."

"I guess it will," Lawson agreed heavily.

"Not that we're such a lawless lot."

"I think the worry stems from Mexico rather than our local folk," Lawson explained. "All you hear about in town is depredations. Garcia — el Leon — has been playing the very devil up and down the river. Mexico is going to end up the real winner in this war — fat on our cows and everything else. The South is in a mess all round, Hugh. I feel now that I ought to have been fighting up there in Virginia long ago."

"Just maybe," Brakes reflected. "It seems to me, if you take on this job of District Marshal, you'll stand about the same chance of getting killed as you would leading a company of men into battle."

"I haven't even thought about it like that," Lawson said disdainfully.

"Perhaps you should, sir," Mrs Dupont put in, glancing at the still untouched cup of tea which she had recently poured for her employer. "Life's all we have, and I've never seen the sense of losing it if it isn't necessary. The young don't take half enough care of their lives."

"It's a valid criticism in its place," Lawson admitted, twitching the tip of a shoulder at his housekeeper. "But I guess life is cheap enough when you come right down to it. This is a matter of doing what's most right. It surely couldn't be wrong to join up with General Lee and the boys in grey."

"Well, me and Mrs Dupont don't have any say in it, boss," Hugh Brakes observed. "It's a decision only you can make."

"Both of them are," Lawson reminded a little darkly. "I'm not going to beard Silas Bolsover right now. Let it run a mite longer. We've done without that damned water up to now, and I guess we can go on doing without it." He didn't add that a vague wish to please, and not offend, Bolsover's wife was also in his mind. "If you want some work for the men, you can build another barn — another horse corral also wouldn't come amiss. The guys who don't like building work can always shuffle off some place else."

"I'll see to it, Mr Lawson," Brakes promised.

"You do that, Hugh," Lawson acknowledged, rising from his chair as the foreman left the room and going to the table nearby on which the tea things stood. Picking up the cup which had been filled for him, he now swallowed to the dregs, pulling a face, for the beverage had got almost cold while he had been talking.

"Let me make a fresh pot," Mrs Dupont suggested.

"No," Lawson said, shaking his head. "I'm not going to sit about in here drinking tea. It's a heck of a time to go to bed, I must agree, but that's where I'm headed. I'm going to catch a good sleep while I've got the chance. Maybe I'll be clear as to what I ought to do when I wake up."

"That sounds very wise," Mrs Dupont said, probably because she felt that she'd got to say something.

Lawson withdrew from the parlour with a bowed head and lagging heels. The house, open to the rafters at its centre, was tall and cool about him, a soaring place which the upper windows facing south filled with shadows and hovering light. Turning left, he walked along the hall to the stairs that ascended the edge of the great well. Moving slowly upwards over the carpeted steps, he watched the motes of dust rocking on the draught which rose towards the top of the sun-layered space. This seemed to have a soporific effect on him, and one yawn after another stretched his jaws. Feeling heavier by the moment, he dragged himself onto the landing which squared about the well; then, after a final walk, entered his room, where he threw off his outer garments and laid himself upon the bed, finding sleep almost at once.

Dreaming, he slept on and on, and there was a voice calling in the world of his slumbers, when he suddenly awoke to the moonlight eddying through the sash window on his right and realized that the voice which he could hear was not calling through his dreams but echoing up to him from the ground outside. The tones were familiar, and he realized that he was listening to

Max Corgan. Max was calling his name insistently, and ordering him with an increasing sharpness to wake up. "Where are you then, Rip van Winkle?" came the final demand.

Rising, on something between a groan and a curse, Lawson staggered to the window and shoved it upwards, thrusting his head and shoulders out into the night air. "Here I am, Lamplighter!" he shouted down caustically. "What's up with you — Castor Oil?"

"Trouble in town, Clem!" came the response.

"The hell-you-say!" Lawson snorted. "How does that concern me?"

"You're the District Marshal designate, aren't you?"

"You big fat rat!"

"Never fat, my friend!"

"What's it all about?"

"Blazeville has had visitors from over the river tonight," Corgan explained. "Somebody must have carried word into Mexico that Roderigo Alvarez had been taken. Anyhow, they've broken Alvarez out of jail. Doc Silk and George Hook are dead."

"Dead!" Lawson cried out in genuine shock. "I can understand about George — But Doc Silk?"

"It seems doc was afraid that wound of Alvarez's was going to mortify," Corgan went on. "Doc went along to the jailhouse just after midnight to change the Mexican's dressings. The rescuers struck at about that time. They gunned down doc and George where they stood. After that they unlocked Alvarez's cell, helped the guy outside, and put him on a waiting horse. Then they all rode off together, going south."

"They're back over the Rio Grande by now."

"I'd put money on it."

"So what can I — or anybody else — do about it, Max?"

"You're not going to allow a strip of water to get in your way?"

"Who says I'm not?" Lawson demanded indignantly. "The river is the international border."

"Are you telling me only the Mexicans can make illegal crossings?"

"You'll get me strung up, Max!"

"You shouldn't take on these jobs."

"I haven't taken on anything, blast you!"

"Now doesn't that sound nice!" Corgan disapproved. "What's Mrs Dupont going to say?"

"You're worse than a fat rat!"

"I told you about that," Corgan returned complacently. "Are you coming?"

Lawson knew that this was the actual moment of decision. Whatever happened, his rest was over for the night. He supposed he'd have to do the job that the town's volunteers required of him, for the pressure both within and without himself now seemed too great to resist. His mind had been almost made up before, but the murders of Virgil Silk and the deputy sheriff had been the clincher. When a party of Mexican bandits became so sure of themselves that they felt they could ride into a Texas town and free one of their own with virtual impunity, it was time for something to be done. It was useless raising questions of selection and who was best fitted any more — no good looking to others in any aspect of it whatsoever. Absolute necessity was now involved, and this was another of those things that he must do as much for himself as everybody else. "Give me a minute to put my clothes on!" he shouted down. "You know where my horse is. If you want to make yourself useful, go and saddle him for me!"

"Yes, sir, Mr Marshal," Corgan replied in a darkie's sing-song.

Lawson was ready to spit blood. That man down there was totally brazen; he had no shame at all. Grinning despite himself, Lawson withdrew to where his garments lay and, finding the moonlight sufficient, dressed himself and strapped on his gun, changing the Colt's cylinder with one from a trouser-pocket and then more than replenishing the pocket with three fully charged cylinders taken from a bottom corner of the nearby wardrobe. After that, lighting a lamp to be on the safe side now, he made his way down through the house and into the kitchen, where he unlocked the back door and stood looking out as Corgan appeared in the sepia gloom of the ranch yard, leading a horse at either hand. "That's the best job you've done all night," Lawson informed his fellow rancher sourly, blowing out the lamp and setting it aside. "I suppose you were still in town, carousing, when the jailbreak took place?"

"Terrible thing," Corgan answered, "I've got to plead virtue for once. I was asleep in the Hotel San Luis when it happened. I had taken a room there. It seemed too far to go home and then come back in the morning."

"Which this now is," Lawson said, stepping out into the yard and shutting the door behind him. "Want to join me in this? You can always catch up with our honourable friends afterwards. It's a long journey north."

"No," Corgan said, relinquishing his hold on Lawson's stallion. "If I'm going north, I'd better go with the rest. It's no good trying to deceive ourselves. Our party could end up two short of its promise, and two would notice."

"That's fair judgment," Lawson said, as they mounted up. "If I'm to do the job, I'd better do it. Start as you mean to go on, eh?"

"Never a bad policy," Corgan allowed. "Glad you don't take it amiss — in the circumstances."

"Heck, no!"

"Then let's get back to town."

They spurred their horses to a trot and headed northeastwards, but they had ridden no further than the front of the bunkhouse when two men stepped out of the dog-trot into their path. Drawing rein, Lawson recognised the long and very erect figure of his foreman and the shorter, much thicker, and perceptibly stooping shape of Ernie Reeve, one of his older ranch hands who had been around so long that he regarded him as permanent staff. "Boys," he greeted carefully. "Something wrong? If that isn't a silly question at this hour."

"Ernie's just galloped in from nightherding over by the river," Hugh Brakes answered. "I figure that what he's just told me amounts to trouble for somebody."

"Go on."

"It was less than an hour ago," Brakes explained. "Ernie here glimpsed a party of horsemen following the river westwards about then. He says they looked like Mexicans. Right, Ernie?"

"Not much doubt they was greasers," Reeve returned. "The moon was glintin' on conchos and such."

"I've had a visitor of my own, Hugh," Lawson said. "Mr Corgan rode over and told me they've had Mexican trouble in Blazeville." He turned his head towards the mounted man on his left. "Do you think the bunch that Ernie Reeve saw could have been the one which freed Roderigo Alvarez from the jailhouse, Max?"

"It's possible," Corgan said doubtfully. "But would it make sense, though? If you're trespassing deliberately, Clem, isn't it usual to leave the dangerous ground by the shortest safe route? That's Uvalde Ford, just four miles from town. Bet your sweet life that's where the men who descended on the jailhouse crossed over from Mexico. I'd expect them to ride home by the same path they used to get here."

"That's what you'd expect all right," Lawson agreed. "So it could be another band. But even if that's so, I guess what it's up to will bear looking into. We might be able to stop something; you never know. If you've got three or four men who're awake and willing, Hugh, get them out here and tell them to saddle up." He glanced round at Corgan again. "Max, I think I'll keep this one in the family."

"Well, there won't be much point

going back to bed just short of sunup," Corgan said. "Clem, I will ride with you this time. I guess my curiosity is whetted. I want to see what happens."

"It could be nothing, Max," Lawson said, looking now at the front of the bunkhouse and the door through which Brakes had just disappeared inside. "There's a lot of country around here, and men soon vanish into it."

The light of a single lamp sprang up inside the sleeping quarters and a certain amount of movement became audible. Around two minutes went by, then a cluster of men emerged from the bunkhouse and hurried towards a nearby corral, the figure of Hugh Brakes clearly visible in the lead. Twisting round in his seat, Lawson watched as the men caught and saddled their horses in the thickening light of the sinking moon, and then he held his restive mount down as the readied animals came surging up to join his own and Corgan's horse. After that, with Corgan and himself to the fore — and Ernie

Reeve and Hugh Brakes riding one at either side of them to form a front rank — he gave the word to ride out.

They cleared the bunkhouse. Now Lawson pulled his stallion's snout out of the east, across southpoint, and almost into the west, heading for the area in which a half triangle of his land thrust back to the Rio Grande and met a similarly shaped piece of graze on Silas Bolsover's 'Rocking Chair' range. Tiny beads of sweat soon formed on Lawson's brow, for the night air had a sultry quality about it, and once or twice he thought he saw electric storms glimmering over the mountains far down in Mexico; but the atmosphere cooled as they neared the Rio Grande, and the gurgling mutter of the waters played through the ashen dusk of moonset, fields of denser shadow settling over the distances up stream where pools ran deep ahead of banks of pale sand and shingle that straggled like visions of the purblind into black nothingness.

The party from the Box L progressed further. It moved steadily westwards against the rio's flow. No word was spoken among the men, and the hoofbeats throbbed dully in the deep soil of the riverside. Out to the right buildings became visible, dim amidst the ranch lamps that shone sentinel over the domestic paths, and Lawson knew that they were riding abreast the Bolsover place. It looked quiet enough across the land, and Lawson hoped that the master and mistress of the ranch were sleeping peacefully in each other's arms, unaware of the furtive doings nearby which had brought their neighbour and his men away from their rest at this ungodly hour of the night.

Lawson pricked with his heels, picking up the pace a little. The riders quickly put the ranch buildings to their rear. Still the character of the land remained the same, and its silent emptiness also. But if it had been all right just to ride up to now — in the hope that something might manifest in line with the possibilities present — a more definite plan was now becoming necessary, for men simply couldn't go on cantering up the river until their horses or their patience gave out.

At risk of trespassing on the 'Rocking Chair' range, a break northwards seemed in order, since any crime planned by the probable marauders that Ernie Reeve had spotted could only be committed within a certain compass and while night covered the land. The compass envisaged must be almost up here, and dawn was no more than an hour or two away. These facts alone must increasingly restrict any evil at present being carried out in the district; and it figured that, short of holing up for the day on this side of the river, any Mexicans operating nearby ought soon to be heading for home — particularly if they meant to make their crossing at the Uvalde Ford, which was now several miles downstream from here.

There was still a trifle of moonglow left. It misted a limited presence behind a black and spiky skyline. A tremor of this light, perhaps more imagined than actual, touched down amidst the waterside shrubs and willows not far ahead. For a split second it seemed to illumine some dissolving ghost of animate form. In the need to shake himself up — and also to be sure — Lawson spurred directly at that vanished remnant of what had appeared to be the spectral and the quick, wondering if a big cat might suddenly spit at his horse or a deer flit away unseen through the foliage along the water's-edge; but instead the movement provoked by his charge was heavier and even faster than he had anticipated.

A horseman leaped from the shadows. Blacker than the river night, he launched himself from the raised ground ahead of Lawson's mount and curved down-wards, his brute's hooves striking amidst stones with a rattle and clatter. After that, splashing into shallow water, the unknown man headed out across the broad stream of the Rio Grande at an amazing full gallop, his wake spitting up like an uneven trail of phosphorescent fire. All the way over he went — served by the same hard bottom and shallow flow for over two hundred yards — and then he dissolved into the great shadow of Mexico and left the briefly disturbed night with no rumour of his passing.

Lawson reined to a stop. The unknown rider had seemed almost to come and go in the snap of a man's fingers. Yet it had not been like that at all. That he had existed there could be no doubt. And it seemed equally sure that he, most probably a Mexican, had had a sound reason for being on the Texas bank of the river. Lawson sensed that the other had been watching and waiting for something. But what? These baffling questions seemed to make up a large part of his existence just now.

5

LAWSON was aware of riders coming to a halt behind and on either side of him as he sat considering the darkened waters which flowed before him.

"Going to cross over, Clem?" Max Corgan asked.

"Maybe," Lawson answered. "I'll swear that fellow we just spooked was watching and waiting for something."

"That's what I'd say too," Corgan commented. "It may have been the Mexicans who freed Alvarez that your man saw. It must have occurred to you that that bunch could have re-entered Mexico at this spot and left the man that you just set running to make sure they weren't being followed out of Texas. Anyhow, this ford is on Silas Bolsover's land and only to be used with his say so. I'd forgotten about it — which I oughtn't to have done — because it's the best ford on this stretch of the Rio Grande. Folk used to drive heavy waggons over it years ago." He sucked his teeth audibly. "Say!"

"What?" Lawson inquired.

"I've just had another thought, Clem," Corgan answered. "There's a Mexican town about three miles the other side of the ford. It's called Convido. There's not much to it, but it did have a church — and a doctor — the last time I was over there."

"A doctor, eh?" Lawson mused, picking up his friend's meaning straightaway. "Alvarez has need of a doctor all right. His rescuers could well have taken him to Convido."

"Do we go and find out?" Corgan asked, hardly concealing a note of command in his question mark.

"I'm going over," Lawson returned. "But I have to be strictly fair about this. Men can't cross international boundaries with impunity. There's a good chance somebody could get hurt or killed over yonder. I can't be responsible for anybody who comes along. If any man is foolish enough to stay with me, it will have to be at his own risk." He let an eye seek his foreman's shape through the gloom. "Hugh, if these hands of ours want to go home, I'll think none the worse of you for taking them there."

"They don't need wet nursing, boss," Brakes said bluntly. "If they want to go, they can find their own way home. I'm coming with you — unless you make it an order the other way round."

"It's a free decision, Hugh, and up to each man as an individual."

"You heard the man, boys," Brakes said. "What's it to be?"

The ranch hands declared as one that they wished to go on.

"Thank you," Lawson said, not without feeling an inner relief. "On your own heads be it. Max?"

"Didn't I start it?" Corgan wondered crossly. "What I do in my life, Clem,

I'm responsible for — and I wouldn't have it otherwise."

"That's plain talk," Lawson conceded. "Let's go then."

First easing their horses to the edge of the raised bank, they jumped the creatures down to the water's-edge, setting up a clash and clatter of stones that was far louder and more sustained than the brief racket which the fugitive had made; and then they urged their mounts into the river and on again, heading for Mexico over a bottom that was indeed rock-firm everywhere and never covered by more than eighteen inches of water.

They arrived soon enough on the opposite bank. Here they paused. They were little more than a stone's throw from the familiar, but Lawson sensed a subtle change in the atmosphere nevertheless. Things alien lay ahead — since the Spanish mind was not the Anglo-Saxon — and Lawson underwent a sudden loss of confidence in himself. Indeed, so pronounced was this that he felt obliged to stress his personal lead, and he bowled an arm forward as he spurred into the black mouth of the steep-walled valley which opened beyond the shore and invited the southbound traveller over what some residual light suggested was a churned up sandy floor that was studded with rocks in places.

But Lawson's brave gesture proved in a sense anti-climactic. The conditions underfoot were not that good; and, after the first surge forward, the night reasserted itself in earnest and forced the party to slow down and ride ahead with much greater care. The valley bottom widened, and the walls spread like arms opening to an emergent starline, while the cold wind off the far uplands blew, chilling sweat and bringing the smells of ancient rock, green water, and the dogrose. There was a sense of being lost, and again a form of paralysis threatened.

Tensed up, Lawson gently lifted and fell with the motion of his horse. That mysterious sixth sense, common to all, but more developed in some men than others, was now profoundly active within him, and he felt trouble not far away. Whether this consciousness of threat concerned him and his companions directly he wasn't sure, but he naturally assumed that these instinctive impulses were coming from ahead; so it came as quite a surprise when his premonition was broken by rumbling noises out of the party's wake and he realized that a herd of cattle was being driven towards them from the river at an altogether unseemly pace. "Do you hear that?" he called, accepting that this, despite his instant and obvious suspicions, was no time to inquire into the whys and wherefores of the business. "Let's get out of the path — before those beeves run us down!"

The horsemen slanted off to the left, where the greater space was located, but even so they reached the containing cliff within fifty yards. Here the company thinned southwards, forming a strip of hidden life that was only one man and beast deep at any point, and shortly after that the rumbling crescendoed into near thunder and vague shapes heaved and lifted in the stygian obscurity of the valley floor close by. Now animals dived and rushed in the vicinity, though even the nearest straggler passed well clear of the concealed Texans, and unseen clouds of dust rose up and filled the air with their choking presence. Then a cracking of stockwhips was audible above the general din, as was the occasional bawling of a Mexican voice, but the herd — no big one — soon cleared the area and went into a pounding recession where its echoes were less and less tightly contained, and presently only a gentle drubbing towards the limit of earshot told that it was still out there and making for the pastures of men growing rich on theft.

"If I'm reading this aright," Corgan announced, after the American band had reassembled itself and was riding back towards what had been taken for the trail, "two Mexican parties have used that ford on the 'Rocking Chair' tonight — since that pack of damned thieves who just passed us couldn't possibly have worked fast enough to have been the men who had been spotted such a short while before heading up the river."

"I go along with that," Lawson said thoughtfully.

"The man who bolted back at the crossing must have been watching for the herd," Hugh Brakes commented. "Sort of marking the spot maybe."

"Maybe," Lawson acknowledged.

"You're going to have to speak to Silas Bolsover, boss," Brakes went on. "He'll have to be put in the know about that ford. It's a loophole on the border that needs blocking pronto. Seems to me these Mexicans come and go as they please — anywhere they like."

"Maybe," Lawson repeated, downright noncommittal this time — and frowning too — for he could not forget whatever it had been that Tina Bolsover had seemed unable to tell him. The worry on that woman's lovely face was for him stamped all over this affair.

"Well, I must admit I feel safer now," Corgan said. "If our runner had had to do with the men who broke Alvarez out of jail, I wouldn't be feeling too happy about approaching Convido now."

"I still don't feel very happy about it," Lawson confessed, "but I guess there's no way anybody can."

Corgan grunted. Here again nothing further was said. The ride into Mexico was resumed. Soon they cleared the valley and came to open grass. Lawson had an impression of the land slipping away southwestwards under the stars. A field of darkness spread across the great hollow. Lawson glimpsed a number of lights at the heart of the darkness, and he smelled woodsmoke. A dog barked too. "Convido?" he asked of Corgan.

"Convido," the other confirmed.

"*Rurales?*"

"There is a post, yes," Corgan answered. "Just two or three men. Or that's how it used to be."

"Yes, we must bear in mind your information is out of date," Lawson said. "Our war could well have caused Mexico City to shift its law closer to the border. There may have been other changes too."

"However that may be," Corgan remarked, "we'll be asking for it if we ride straight into the town square."

"Leave our horses outside?"

"That's the idea," Corgan approved. "We can then break up into two parts and sneak into town to find out what's doing. There's no need to show ourselves where it could be dangerous to be seen."

Lawson turned his face prayerfully to heaven. "May it prove that easy, Max."

They followed what was now a clearly defined trail into a right-hand bend. Beyond the corner, they passed down the land and the few lights of

Convido quickly drew closer. Within ten minutes they reached a stand of tulip trees which grew about a hundred yards short of the town's eastern side. Here they dismounted and tied their horses among the boles, and the trees stirred softly above them while they drew together and discussed briefly what they were going to do.

Lawson listened to everybody who spoke; then, drawing on the consensus, he said the main idea was to seek any property — excluding the cantinas — which had a number of horses standing outside it. They were also to try to locate the town jailhouse and find out how many lawmen were present. Any matters which seemed to relate to these two interests were to be investigated according to opportunity. The whole business was obviously loose and impromptu, yet could hardly be more since, when it came right down to it, the Texans could not be really sure that their Mexican quarry had come to this place. Indeed, when what they were doing was carefully examined, Lawson knew that the margin for error was high and that their journey over the Rio Grande could still prove to be a disastrous folly.

Now the party divided. Brakes took the men who had joined him from the Box L's bunkhouse into the southern half of Convido, while Lawson, Corgan and Ernie Reeve, entered the northern, their movements not unduly furtive, for there was nobody about and even the monotonous barking of the dog which they had heard from outside town appeared to be an accepted and normal thing.

As they went along, Lawson asked Corgan if he could remember where the doctor had lived in Convido when last he was there. Corgan answered that he could not be sure, but seemed to recall having been told that *el medico* lived on this side of the town and in a rather splendid red-tiled dwelling, with doors and balconies of the Moorish type. This house stood near the church.

"Show us when we get there," Lawson requested.

They groped their way down an alley or two and along the edges of several fruit groves and planted gardens. Adobe walls enclosed patios on their left, and generally darkened casements peered blindly down on them out of brickwork that was covered with flowering creepers. Nor was it that romantic, for stinging insects hummed, bullfrogs burped, and crickets made a racket that was all their own. The night was sticky, too, down here beneath the mountain wind.

Presently they approached the western end of the town. Here one or two bigger houses had their places, and the Spanish church threw up the silhouette of its bell-tower against the lower stars. Moving to the rear of the properties still, Lawson had a fair view down the length of each in turn and saw finally that a lamp was burning in what appeared to be a large room near the back of the house next to

108

the church. "Max?" Lawson prompted, sensing uncertainty in his friend.

"That could be it," Corgan said. "Let's creep up and have a peep in."

They closed in on tiptoe, encountering neither dug earth nor any other form of obstruction between them and the lighted window. Then, the three of them crouching at the lower left-hand corner of the glass, Lawson lifted the top of his head and looked into the room beyond. What he saw startled him momentarily breathless, and he found it hard to credit that it had all been so easy. For there, stripped to the waist and with his right hand and forearm heavily bound, was Roderigo Alvarez. The killer was sitting on a scrub-topped table, and beside him stood a balding, proud-featured man, with a spade-beard and a pair of highly intelligent-looking brown eyes. To judge from the befrilled elegance of his white silk shirt, red cummerbund, and perfectly tailored black drainpipe trousers, he was the doctor, but elsewhere in the room stood several individuals of far less refined appearances. They were swarthy, poorly dressed, and generally mean-featured and unkempt. They were also armed to the teeth and covered with the dust of travel.

These fellows, naturally favouring the description of *bandidos*, were topped by one who was obviously their leader. This man — no less muddy-eyed and hard-mouthed than the rest — was otherwise rather splendid to look upon; for, inbred to his great height were proportionate width of shoulder and depth of chest, and he had too the lean, square hips of one born naturally strong. His roundness of limb confirmed the rest of his physical opulence, and his colouring was tawny and strangely feral. Lawson had seen the other a few times before — in various circumstances — and knew him for Alfredo Garcia, the self-styled Lion of Mexico and Scourge of the Rio Bravo. Nobody could deny that the huge Mexican looked the part.

Though able to pick out voices, the spying Lawson could not hear what was actually being said — his own Spanish was not up to following rapidly spoken patois and colloquialisms — and the best understanding he could reach of what was happening within was that an argument was taking place. There were various gestures included, and these hinted that el Leon and company wanted to take Alvarez with them at the present time while the doctor wished to hang on to him, most probably for further treatment. There was nothing angry about the exchanges, for the medical man was obviously accorded great respect, and it appeared that he won the day, for Alfredo Garcia suddenly grinned and threw up his hands in submission, speaking words to Alvarez that brought a tired nod and an evident entire willingness to co-operate with both authorities concerned. "Back!" the watching Lawson now hissed at his companions — explaining in a few hasty words what he had just witnessed.

111

"I think they'll be leaving from the rear of the house!"

In fact he proved wrong about that. For, after he and his two companions had retreated into a pool of darkness behind the next dwelling in line, he heard a door open at the front of the doctor's home and the still talking Garcia and his men leave in what sounded like an orderly enough fashion, a slow clip-clopping of hooves a few moments later suggesting that they were leading their horses towards some building nearby — perhaps a *cantina* — and were going to rest up for what was left of the night where drink and women were to be found.

"So Alvarez is still in there?" Corgan queried.

"I believe so," Lawson replied.

"Figure we can fish him out?"

"I suspect that's what we're here for," Lawson returned.

"I'm not riding back to Blazeville empty-handed, Clem," Corgan said grimly. "Alvarez has a date with the hangman, and I want to see he keeps it. I don't aim to waste this journey."

"My feelings exactly," Lawson agreed, though his more cautious nature was already weighing the pros and cons. "But we're going to have to be as patient as we are careful about it. I imagine *el medico* yonder intends putting Alvarez to bed. Let's hope he puts him into a room downstairs. If he doesn't, life could get a shade harder than we like. Even impossible! We'll have to think hard before we go trespassing deep into the doctor's house. If the alarm goes up, I fear our goose is cooked. We're too far from our horses to reach them and get away alive."

"All right, Clem," Corgan said, "we've heard you. Let's give it a shot anyhow."

Once more they advanced on the lighted window towards the back of the doctor's house, and again Lawson peeped inside. He saw that Alvarez and the man wearing the red cummberbund were still occupying much the same positions that he had seen them in before. The seated Alvarez was considering his bandaged arm and nodding mechanically as the doctor spoke to him in an earnest voice.

The talk showed signs of continuing and, ducking low, Lawson moved aside and gave his companions a chance to look in at the window. Then, a few minutes later — when Lawson was again at the glass — the doctor steadied Alvarez off his table seat and led him to a door in the back of the room which the pair occupied. The door was opened wide, and left standing so after the two men had passed through it. Lawson was able to see into the room beyond. This contained an iron cot and one or two other pieces of simple furniture. He had no doubt it was here that the wounded man was to be given the extra rest and treatment that he needed, and again he moved aside so that Corgan and Ernie Reeve could see what was happening within.

"He shouldn't be too difficult to reach in there, Clem," Corgan whispered. "There must be somewhere we can enter at the back of the house."

"Through a locked door?" Lawson murmured dryly. "Or do we put a window out?"

"You sassing me, mister?" Corgan asked.

"We can't afford to make the slightest sound," Lawson reminded. "I believe the front door must still be unlocked. We can get in through that, then hide up until the doctor goes to bed. We'll worry about how to get out again when we've taken Alvarez prisoner."

"All right," Corgan said. "That sounds good to me. Let's be quick about it."

Lawson gave the lead. He made for the eastern corner at the front of the house. Rounding it, he catfooted towards the front door which a hanging light showed to be set back in the wall behind the middle of three Moorish arches that supported the roof of the verandah that ran across the face of the dwelling. All too aware that anybody watching from the square must have spotted his presence by now, Lawson ignored the possibility of an alarm being raised and opened the doctor's front door, entering swiftly and standing then with the woodwork held back just enough for his two companions to slip in also. After that he closed the door silently behind them.

They stood now among the slender columns of a tessellated hall. There was an area of darkness immediately before them, but a lighted doorway shone at the rear of the blackness and provided a line of vision right through to what Lawson judged would be the part of the house into which he and his friends had recently peered to see *el medico* and Alvarez speaking together. Despite Lawson's earlier comment on the need to hide up, once indoors, they inched instinctively towards the light, and it was only the sudden noise of movement at the further end of the house that caused them to check instantly and stand motionless. The rather dashing figure of the doctor entered the distant lamplight from an unseen area on the left, and the man paused and looked towards the darkness, but he plainly had no idea that intruders had entered the front of the house and just as quickly passed into another unseen area of the lower room, reappearing soon afterwards with a candle burning in a silver stick. Hesitating again, he cast a glance around him; then, apparently satisfied that all was well, advanced towards the darkness, leaving the lamp burning in his wake — doubtless to facilitate any movement that his patient might need to make during the remainder of the night — and Lawson nudged his friends over to the right and went with them, allowing the blackness at the extreme edge of the hall to cloak them against the feebleness of the candlelight in the degree that it could.

The doctor entered the hall, and the

spluttering candleglow did little more than light his steps and striding figure. Going straight to the door, he turned the key, removing this from the lock and placing it on a brass plate that stood on top of a table to the right of the door. After that he made for a stairway on the same side of the hall and began climbing towards the floor above. The noise from his ascent soon ceased, though there were other sounds through the ceiling as he prepared for and got into bed; but a pindrop silence presently descended on the house and the intruders were able to stir again with little risk of being heard.

Lawson rummaged out a match. Striking this, he held up the tiny flame and went over to where the key lay upon the plate. Then he unlocked the front door again. "Okay," he breathed at his companions, who had moved back into the middle of the hall and were waiting for him to rejoin them, "we know now where we'll be leaving from."

As ever, Corgan was impatient to be doing. He picked up the lead. Lawson and Reeve tiptoed behind him towards the lighted room beyond the dark. Into this room they passed, and Lawson saw immediately from the furnishings that it was the doctor's surgery and the place where Roderigo Alvarez had been treated. On the left, Lawson also saw the doorway through which the patient had been shown. He tensed himself for action, watching as Corgan drew and cocked his revolver; then he joined the surge forward as the lean-featured Corgan threw open Alvarez's door and burst inside, entering a darkened place — though the light from the surgery all too dimly revealed the iron cot on which the wounded Mexican was now struggling up. "Not a murmur!" Corgan warned. "Get out of bed!"

Alvarez threw back the bedclothes. It was then that Lawson saw the Mexican's left hand held a gun.

6

IT seemed then that everything was happening at once. Fire streaked, hammers bit and powder roared, and a voice uttered a long, thin scream. Plucking out his own gun, Lawson was aware of somebody sitting down hard and then of Alvarez's revolver pointing directly at him. A bullet whipped his left cheekbone, stinging like fury, and another tore through the slack of his jacket's right shoulder, causing the entire garment to jump alarmingly on his back.

He replied reflexively, aiming at the middle of the torso behind the Mexican's gunflashes. Alvarez shuddered visibly, and Lawson had the impression of blood flying. But the man shot at him again — determined as ever — and this time the lead creased a little deeper, burning across the top of his left leg.

The voice of his subconscious warned in a split second that his chances had run out. This time he had got to finish it before the Mexican finished him.

He raised the muzzle of his Colt a fraction and began to fan the hammer, chopping a series of blasts out of the weapon, and his ears were filled with roaring echoes, while flaring powder grains arced back and burned his hands. Now he gagged on the bitter stench of the explosives, and blinked the dazzle out of his eyes; but the fire from the man opposite had ceased; and, as a window roiled into the gunsmoke present, he saw Alvarez flung back over the head of the cot. The Mexican's bared chest was shot full of holes and leaking darkly, and his newly dead eyes were fixing. "God-damn you!" Lawson raged, and he meant just that.

A hand shook roughly at his arm. "It's Mr Corgan!" Ernie Reeve insisted. "Sir — he's bad hurt!"

For a moment the ranch hand's words had little meaning. Lawson stood there shaking. Then he broke the empty cylinder out of his Colt and, going to his pocket, replaced it with another that was loaded all round. After that he gazed down to his right, a sudden horror filling him at what he saw, for Max Corgan was doubled into the angle formed by the floor and the wall, blood spilling through the fingers which he had pressed to a chest wound that looked dangerously close to his heart. "Oh, no!" he roared. "Not that!"

Corgan tried to look up, but couldn't manage it. "They'll be — two short in — in Virginia," he whispered.

"Hang on, Max!" Lawson pleaded, almost panicking.

There was no reply from Corgan.

"He's dead," Ernie Reeve said.

"Don't talk like a fool, man!" Lawson snapped at the other. "Stir your stumps, Ernie! Get that front door open for me!"

Nodding, Reeve took off fast.

Then, palming his gun away, Lawson bent and, putting an arm through

Corgan's fork and pulling the inert man's left hand around his neck, he heaved his friend across his shoulders. Now, manoeuvring deftly, he carried Corgan's limp form out of the bedroom and ran up the floor of the surgery beyond, re-entering the darkness of the hall and making for the front door, where he had an impression of Ernie Reeve standing against an oblong of dim greyness that could only be the first glimmer of the coming dawn.

"*Que suceder?*" a man's voice shouted down the stairs. "*Deseaba usted algo?*"

"That's a hell of a question, doctor!" Lawson gritted in the direction of the unseen man on the floor above. "*Siento molestarle, senor!*"

But Ernie Reeve had another and far more discouraging way of answering *el medico*. He fired a couple shots towards the foot of the stairs. One of the slugs ricocheted upwards, and the man at the top of steps went audibly into full retreat.

Lawson passed outside. Checking,

he gave the man upon his shoulders a little chuck in order to make a more comfortable burden of him. Then he moved away from the house and into Convido's just visible square. Here he turned left, conscious of an upstairs window opening in the dwelling adjacent and the doctor's voice shouting: "*Socorro! Socorro! Ladrons — ladrons!*"

Nothing happened. *El médico* went on shouting, but nobody appeared on the street. Indeed, it seemed that hardly a face looked out. Lawson guessed that everybody in town was still asleep or unprepared to answer the cries for help. He ran steadily onwards, thanking heaven for his strong back and legs, for Corgan's weight had bothered him little as yet, and he found that he could easily keep level with the unburdened Ernie Reeve who had come up from the rear and was now running at his right elbow.

But it couldn't last. They had barely left the eastern edge of the square, when a shouting broke out among those in town who were now fully alerted. Questions flew back and forth and, with a true understanding arrived at — something which didn't take so very long — a rifle exploded behind the fugitives and a bullet cut up the dust near Lawson's feet. He swore to himself, and was greatly tempted to turn aside into the alleys and gardens at the rear of the white-walled houses on the left of the street which he and Reeve had just entered, but he realized that, though this might increase their safety in the short term, the advantage could soon be lost through the indirect manner in which they would be forced to approach their horses. No, allowing that the chances of being hit in the present light were minimal — and that Reeve and he would undoubtedly cover the ground much faster if they stuck to the direct route out of town — he believed their hopes of making good what must still be regarded as an unlikely escape would be enhanced if they went on as they were at present.

A few more gunshots rang out behind them, but no bullet passed near enough to worry about. Then, as they came to the boundary of the town, figures dashed in from the right and got between them and the firing. Lawson recognised Hugh Brakes's shape in the phantom light that quivered down the east, and had the impression that the larger half of their party had finished exploring their part of the town a good while ago and been waiting for him and the other two to reappear at a position from which they could watch all possible routes of emergence from this quarter of Convido. "What's happened to Mr Corgan, boss?" Brakes panted from behind Lawson's head.

"We found what we were looking for," Lawson gasped in reply, "but caught more than we bargained for. He stopped a bullet."

"He's dead," Ernie Reeve put in. "Never saw a hombre deader!"

"Drop him, boss!" Brakes advised.

"It's your hide that matters!"

"Some excuse!" Lawson snarled, putting in a spurt and refusing to listen to any more.

The tulip trees which concealed the horses showed ahead, and the tops of their beautiful shapes swept gracefully back and forth in the dawn wind. Reaching the boles, the men from the Box L dived among them and freed their horses. Panting heavily by this time, Lawson cast Corgan's frame across the man's own saddle and, with this done, Hugh Brakes made a rapid examination of the shot rancher. "Ernie's right, boss," he said. "This man is dead."

"I don't give a damn for that!" Lawson retorted. "He belongs to Texas, and in Texas ground he'll lie!"

"He needs to be tied on," Brakes warned. "This is going to be a hard ride — "

Just then a mighty voice started bellowing at the centre of Convido. Everybody among the tulip trees gave an ear. Lawson knew they were listening to Alfredo Garcia. El Léon was inviting the people of the town to join him in pursuit of the intruders. Whatever happened there, a chase was about to begin. There was no more time to lose. It wasn't all that far back to the border, but it would indeed be a hard ride. "Shut up, Hugh!" he ordered. "Let's get the hell out of here!"

The ranch hands jinked clear of the tulip trees. Coming to the trail, they dug in their spurs and went galloping up the land. Struggling to control Corgan's horse as well as his own, Lawson immediately found himself more hampered than he had expected and bringing up the rear. But he stuck to his task, increasingly out of pure stubbornness — since his common sense told him that shock and grief had caused him to behave a little irrationally up to now — and he managed to get going fairly smoothly, though the riders ahead of him soon opened up a gap that seemed to yawn in the slowly improving visibility of the dawn hour.

Reaching the top of the climb away from Convido, Lawson bore round to the left — slowing to help Corgan's horse to accurately track his own — and then let out northwards, throwing an anxious glance back across his shoulder as he once more got the horses running smoothly. The pursuit was there, and well in sight too. A dozen Mexicans were coming up the hill, heads down and reins threshing. He didn't like the look of it. His own men were already two hundred yards ahead of him. He was travelling too slowly. The second horse was holding his own back. He ought to release it in his own interests. Yet despite being virtually certain in himself that Max Corgan was dead, he kept hanging on to the hope that there might still be life left in the man, and he simply could not abandon him to the short shrift that he would surely get from el Léon.

The first gunshots cracked out in the dawn silence. They cast a roll of harsh echoes back to the unseen skylines. Lawson heard one piece of lead spit by and another whimper as it fell. Raking his own horse, he bawled at the other, conscious that he was still being slowly overtaken by the chase. Other weapons cracked and banged, a rifle adding its heavier boom to the windy snap and roar of the cap-and-ball pistols in more general use. Lawson's back began to feel horribly vulnerable. True, the guns were letting rip at him from around maximum range, but a lucky bullet fired from three or four hundred yards could kill just as surely as one fired from thirty. The trick was to stay out of gunshot altogether, and at present he wasn't achieving it.

Then fortune played a hand. Corgan's horse, evidently burned by lead, let out a shrill whinny and bucked and kicked. From the corner of his eye, Lawson saw the unsecured body that it was carrying go flying into the air and fall at the trailside, where it spun over a couple of times before coming to rest and lying motionless. Perceiving that it would be nothing short of suicidal to halt and try to retrieve matters, Lawson did what was obviously the only sane thing in the circumstances and released the reins by which he had been towing Corgan's mount. The creature at once fell back, and Lawson's stallion took a fillip — surging ahead at a pace which no other animal present on either side could match. A minute later the guns ceased to shoot behind him, and shortly after that he was riding among his own men once more.

Now the valley that led to the river started to absorb the fugitives, and Lawson found that his eyesight was less trustworthy than it had been before. Despite being set wide apart at this southern end, the walls of rock kept out much of the dawnlight and darkened the floor. This forced Lawson and his companions to slow down, for there were enough rocks scattered across their path to form a hazard which had to be treated with respect. Inevitably, as the fugitives cut back on their pace, so the men chasing them derived the full benefit of being able to still ride flat out, and they soon reduced the gap and were able to begin shooting again.

The echoes of the firing multiplied and dinned at Lawsons's eardrums. Deeper into the gradually narrowing valley pounded the chase. Ricochets spat and hummed. Suddenly one of the Box L cowboys threw up his arms and toppled backwards out of his saddle. He came to rest upon his back, lying in his employer's path, and Lawson lifted his horse over the shot man, fearing the worst as he saw the fixed eyes in the other's ashen face.

This success seemed to inspire the Mexicans.

Their firing intensified still more; in fact it grew quite wild. Now the reverberations of shot and hoof pulsed along the clifftops and seemed to set the valley quaking. The air was full of lead, but nobody else was hit and, as the following guns must be emptying fast and reloading them in the saddle was very difficult, Lawson began to hope that he and what was left of his party might regain Texas without disaster becoming total, but then the trapped vibrations brought down a huge shower of stones upon their heads from a deeply eroded strip of the western rimrock.

Enclosed by hurtling rocks, Lawson rode on in the breathtaking expectation of being struck from his saddle at any instant; but, though he saw bounding masses tear Reeve and two other men from the backs of their mounts, he passed through the granite shower unscathed — as did Hugh Brakes also — and after that they were able to ride on for a minute in relative safety while the pursuers, checked by the fall of rock in their path — as Lawson's quick glance round showed — rode wide of the blockage and almost out to the valley's eastern wall before swinging back to regain the trail and resume the chase.

The northern end of the valley appeared up front. Lawson and Brakes passed through it. Over the shore they pounded and into the river itself, splashing towards the thin mists that hung above the centre of the flow. Again the hard bottom carried the horses forward without difficulty, but the riders were only about two thirds of the way across the river when the shooting started once more. Lawson picked up the flitting passage of a slug near his right ear. He sensed that the shot had been carefully aimed by somebody who was tired of the wild firing that had gone before and now meant business. Looking back again, he saw that the Mexicans had reined in on the southern shore and that el Léon himself held a repeating rifle to his shoulder and was blasting away systematically at the escapers. Lawson wished to heaven that the river mist was thicker and more off-putting to the marksman, and he wished it still more when Brakes was suddenly lifted forward onto his mount's neck — as if chucked there by a powerful hand — and then jolted back into place looking terribly shocked. Clearly the foreman had been hit, but he kept spurring on.

"How bad is it?" Lawson called.

Brakes's face came round, features wrenched with agony. He tried to speak, but the words wouldn't come. Not that they were needed, for Lawson could see that the other had been severely hurt.

Further shots pursued those already fired. The bullets missed by little enough, but miss they did. Then the fugitives cleared the river and drove their horses up the Texas bank. Now the gunfire ceased again. Lawson prayed that this meant the Mexicans were going to respect the border on this occasion and accept that the two surviving Texans had escaped. He craned in the hope of seeing el

Léon and company turn away from Rio Grande and start back for Convido. But his heart sank within him as he saw that the Mexicans were coming on and clearly ready to enter a new stage of the hunt. Thus their lack of respect for authority in war-reduced Texas was again being demonstrated, and Lawson felt the acute frustration of knowing that there wasn't much that the people on this side of the river could do about it.

Lawson's attention was called back to Brakes. Wounded the man might be, but it was obvious that his head was still clear, for he had set off down the bank of the river and was following the first of the routes back to the Box L. Heading after the other, Lawson studied the foreman's posture in the saddle. He could see that Brakes was not going to make it home. He reckoned the man had perhaps another three miles of riding left in him, then he was going to fall off his horse and it would all come down to a futile last stand — if that rifle of el Léon's did not settle the matter somewhat before that.

This business had now to be viewed in the light of strict common sense. If Brakes and he tried to see this through alone they were going to die. But there ought to be help nearby. Silas Bolsover's 'Rocking Chair' ranch house stood within two miles of this spot. He would take Brakes there. It was difficult to imagine that Alfredo Garcia would risk attacking the home of a major rancher on this side of the river. After all, he had nothing more to gain from it than the deaths of the two remaining members of an *Americano* party that had dared to cross the Rio Grande and put paid to one of his *bandidos*. Revenge might be sweet, but the price always had to be considered, and the cost of attacking the Bolsover home buildings could well run out too high before all was done. For, though the law over here was woefully short of men, the Texas Rangers still existed and, if they were finally sent in against el Léon, they would do a thoroughly ruthless job along this stretch of the Rio Grande and reap an abundant harvest of rope fruit.

Lawson drove his mount to another spurt. He drew level with his foreman's right elbow. The now rapidly improving light showed him that Brakes's wound might be less serious than he had feared. The man had been shot high behind the left shoulder. Judging from the bloodstains present, the bullet had gone in at the back and come out at the front. The danger was, of course, that the collar-bone had been broken — which would account for the great shock and pain that had been present — but, unless hit again, Brakes appeared unlikely to die this day or for many a day yet. "I'm going to take you to the Bolsover place, Hugh!" Lawson called across.

"You sure about that?" Brakes asked in a strained voice. "Will Silas stand for it?"

"He'd better!" Lawson snorted. "We're in a crisis, man!"

"We could be taking him trouble, boss."

"That's a risk we have to take," Lawson retorted. "But I don't think we need fear that. Alfredo Garcia knows how many beans make five."

"I hope you're right."

The chimneys of the Bolsover ranch house had become visible above the land. Now Lawson craned over his shoulder for the umpteenth time. He saw at once that the Mexicans had lost a good deal of ground in recent minutes. Between their pause on the southern bank of the river — and what must have been a much slower crossing — they had fallen back by at least a quarter of a mile and were now riding well out of gunshot. Indeed, their horses appeared to be labouring and it seemed unlikely that the chase would again become a threat to life and limb before the two fleeing Americans reached the ranch yard of the 'Rocking

Chair'. Nevertheless, believing that luck should receive practical encouragement, Lawson swerved in closer to the horse galloping beside his own and delivered a whack on the rump that kept the foreman's mount running at top speed and, lifting over the slight ridge ahead, they slanted left across the land beyond and made for the cluster of buildings that formed the headquarters of the Bolsover spread.

The structures loomed swiftly and, noticing a sudden slight loss of control in his wounded companion, Lawson seized Brakes's horse at the bit and steered it round the southern end of the house and into the ranch yard. There was little going on as yet, but a smell of cooking nearby told that the crew's breakfast was already in preparation. Fearing to halt too soon, Lawson kept the horses moving and didn't actually stop until the brutes had their noses within two yards of the Bolsover back door. Then, though he had expected to see the master of the 'Rocking

Chair' pretty soon, he was startled into a yelp as Silas Bolsover's dark and not unhandsome head thrust out of the kitchen window adjacent and, teeth still chewing toast, bellowed an impolite inquiry as to what his fellow rancher was doing outside his house at this 'blasted hour of the morning'.

"Hugh Brakes has been shot," Lawson explained, "and we're being chased by Alfredo Garcia and his *bandidos*. We need your help — and protection."

"Are you mad, Lawson?" Bolsover roared. "Turn round, will you, and ride the hell out of here!"

"Not a chance, Silas!" Lawson retorted flatly.

"My men are hardly out of their beds!"

"To blazes with that!" Lawson bit in return. "Just let Hugh and me indoors!"

"No!"

"Yes!" cried a woman's voice from behind the man. "Get in here, Clem, and bring Hugh Brakes with you!"

"That's more like it!" Lawson declared, swinging down fast and then helping Brakes off his horse at the best pace their joint effort could bring about.

But they still weren't to get inside the house, for the crippled Silas Bolsover — known rather callously around the district as 'Clubfoot' — had just emerged from the kitchen door, a glowering, strong-jawed figure who, at six and a half feet in height, topped Lawson and Brakes, both tall men themselves, by several inches. Possessing, too, a fine spread of chest and shoulders, he blocked the entrance at his back entirely as he looked across the ranch yard with a steely gaze that was nevertheless shadowed by what Lawson read as a kind of outraged despair. Putting up a hand, the big cripple began to make shooing movements and Lawson turned his head and saw that the pursuing Mexicans had reached the eastern edge of the ranch yard, slowed their horses to a walk, and were now advancing in the wake of el Léon, who was grinning at Bolsover's feeble gestures and clearly had no intention of obeying them.

Lawson reached for his gun, hoping to prompt Silas Bolsover into a similar warlike movement, but the crippled giant reached down with his left hand and smothered the smaller man's draw, still staring fixedly at el Léon but offering no explanation as to why he would not consider any form of offensive action against the equally big Alfredo Garcia. "Go away, damn your eyes!" he rasped, though almost pleading. "That's all you've got to do — just go away!"

"But, *senor*," Garcia pleaded silkily, "does eet not shame you to treat a friend thus?"

"Since when were you a friend of mine?" Bolsover demanded brusquely.

"How can you say that to one who has the freedom of your land?" el Léon appealed. "One, honoured *senor*, who pays you generously for the privilege?"

"That's the end of me, Garcia," Bolsover said thickly. "What good's that to you?"

"So foolish!" the big Mexican gently scoffed. "I would not do this theeng. I weesh only to bind us closer in our friendship, senor. That man — Clem Lawson, is eet not? — has earned death. You shall help me keel him, and the deed will sanctify our *armistad*. What ees yours weel be mine, and I shall pay you no more." He waited, grinning. "Ees that not so?"

"Literally, you'll know where the body's buried, eh?" Bolsover inquired bitterly. "No, I'm not going to let you blackmail me, Garcia! I'll see you at the devil first!"

"Heh, heh, heh," el Léon chuckled. "*El diablo* ees in no hurry for me, honoured *senor*. It weel be your neck in the noose eef Lawson is permeeted to ride free and tell your people what he now knows concerning you. Oh, such scandal! El Léon rides into Texas over the 'Rocking Chair' *vado*, and

144

back he goes again the same. *Vamos — Mejico!* It is thus that he ees not caught."

"You fiend!" Bolsover breathed, though his head went down submissively. "What is it you want?"

"I have told you, honoured *senor.*"

"Cut out that bullshit!" Bolsover roared, slamming his right fist into the palm of his left hand. "Clem Lawson is an important man in this part of Texas. I can't kill him out of hand. It's one thing to blow his foreman's brains out, but quite another — "

Lawson perceived an extreme need to take the initiative before it was too late. He made another attempt to draw his revolver. Bolsover promptly dropped him with a quick uppercut. He whipped out his own gun as Lawson hit the ground. "For God's sake behave, Clem!" he warned. "We're in a cleft stick!"

"Eet ees so," Garcia agreed, nodding with an air of great profundity. "You keep good wheesky, Silas. I dreenk some. We go to your study and talk of this theeng."

"Very well," Bolsover said shortly. Then he disarmed Lawson and Brakes, thrusting their weapons into the top of his trousers. "Get up, Clem; you aren't hurt. Garcia, tell your people to leave."

"My people weel stay," el Léon responded. "They do not like to be far separated from their chefe. It makes them — *nervioso*." His sinister laugh sounded again. "What harm weel they do? It does not matter who sees. *Mejico* and Texas are not at war."

"At that," Bolsover growled, watching as the risen Lawson brushed himself down, "I suppose they could be anybody and here for any reason. Light, Garcia, and come on in. You, too, Clem. And take care of Hugh Brakes. He appears ready to faint off."

"Do you wonder?" Lawson asked shakily, using his left shoulder to support Brakes. "He's probably got a

146

busted collar-bone. To make matters worse, Garcia and those murdering hellions of his did for Doc Silk when they were in Blazeville last night. What other medical help is there around?"

Bolsover shrugged dismissively, the muzzle of his revolver twitching towards the back door. "Too bad. But it's all in a lifetime, mister. We've got bigger fish to fry."

Lawson helped Brakes over the doorstep and into the Bolsover kitchen. He saw the rancher's wife sitting at her breakfast table. She was holding a cup of coffee between her hands and just short of her lips. Tina Bolsover's face was pale but expressionless. She had obviously heard every word that had been spoken outside the back door and must have a clear idea of what was happening. "Good morning, Tina," Lawson said. "I understand now."

She said nothing.

"I understand now," he repeated,

"what you could not bring yourself to tell me down there at the pond."

Still the woman said nothing.

A big palm landed between Lawson's shoulder-blades and shoved him onwards.

7

THEY entered Bolsover's study a minute later, and Lawson — who had never been there before — had to admit to himself that it was a singularly elegant room. Silas must have laid out a small fortune on the oak panelling, a like sum on the carved rosewood desk and leather armchairs and such — all of which had that heavily comfortable English look about them — and the full amount on the paintings and shelves of books around the walls.

Like most folk regarding the huge, hopping cripple as a man, Lawson had always supposed Bolsover to be a person of little education and less taste; but then one could so easily be wrong in these judgments. Tina had not married the fellow on a whim. A staunch believer in that old adage concerning 'birds of a feather', Lawson had long been certain that life had threads of inevitability woven into it, and that folk only found their own as they progressed through it. Not that Bolsover was anything very wonderful; but then Tina wasn't perfect either — as didn't Lawson have reason to know.

"Have a seat, Garcia," Bolsover invited, going to a drinks table and pouring a stiff jolt of a potent-looking whisky from a cut-glass decanter into a tumbler. "Oh, there are cigars in the box on my desk. Help yourself if you fancy one." He tossed back a brief laugh. "Excuse me if I don't indulge. It's too early for me. Coffee is more my mark at this hour."

"It wouldn't do Hugh and me any harm either," Lawson remarked, getting about the reaction he expected, when Bolsover threw a withering glance at him and told him to shut up.

"Okay," Lawson responded, smiling wryly at Brakes. "I'll remember this if you ever come calling over at my place."

"Stop playing the buffoon, Lawson!" Bolsover ordered coldly. "It isn't like you. There'll be no calling — and well we both know it. Whistling in the dark, eh?"

Lawson gave his unoccupied shoulder a shrug. It could be that Bolsover had just made a valid point. Perhaps he was looking for courage from anywhere that he could find it. He had fought a number of times in his life, and been in a few tight spots, but it had always been him against another in open battle — or against circumstances that he could weigh up and counter — and he had always been buoyed by the knowledge that his skill or strength would determine the outcome; but here he was the essential victim — the prisoner of two ruthless men who had left themselves no choice but to murder him by one means or another. To be thus at the mercy of his enemies was a whole new experience, and it did bring a chill to his blood. Yet he said nonchalantly: "I guess we'll have to wait and see who has the last whistle."

"Of thees you make too much," Garcia commented, unseated still and pacing as he knocked back the whisky that his host had recently handed him. "Ah, good!" He drew up an eye and the corner of his mouth, giving his head a tiny shake to emphasize that the liquor had hit the spot. "I would shoot heem now."

"I'd *like* to shoot him now," Bolsover amplified viciously. "But I've got a crew outside who're plenty smart enough, and a wife in the kitchen who's far too smart. I have to watch what I do."

"You'd have to be mighty careful of Tina," Lawson agreed.

"What do you know about it?" Bolsover inquired aggressively.

"I knew her first, Silas," Lawson reminded, giving his voice a faint inflection, for he was determined to worry and unsettle the other — as a matter of policy — by any means he could.

"What the hell's that supposed to mean?" Bolsover asked sharply.

"Anything you like," Lawson replied quietly. "Anything at all."

"You be careful, Clem," Bolsover hissed. "You be very careful."

"Good as dead, am I not?"

"*Americanos*," Garcia mourned. "Would you have me die of thirst, honoured senor?"

"I told you to cut that out, Alfredo!" Bolsover blazed, pushing the cut-glass decanter into the Mexican's hand and gesturing for him to help himself. "I can do without you sassing me when I'm getting something worse from that stinking Don Juan!"

"True, true," Lawson mused. "Women have always been a serious business with me. How about you, Silas? Straight for the petticoat, eh? But, of course, that foot of yours has always slowed you up a bit."

"If you're hinting at what I think

you're hinting at," Bolsover seethed, "I'll lynch you!"

"So, so," el Léon interrupted. "You would hang heem? Indulge yourself, honoured — " he grinned insultingly — "my friend. He has a barn. You have a rope. Of beams there are plenty."

"What's that you're suggesting?" Bolsover demanded.

"Men grow tired of life," Garcia answered, pouring himself a third and very large whisky. "Sometimes they hang themselves. They go to the barn and — " He raised his left hand, making a fist but keeping the index finger extended at the horizontal; then he caused the tip of the finger to dip abruptly and quiver. "So — eet ees all over."

"I get you, you devil!" Bolsover exclaimed in what was plainly an instant of horrified revelation. "String him up in my barn; then carry him to his own barn — dead — and hang him up again there. Who'd ever know what happened? Who could ever know?"

"Nobody," Garcia said simply; and, with a wicked leer, he poured what was left of his host's whisky into the tumbler and set the empty decanter down on the drinks table.

"Yeah," Bolsover admitted rather grudgingly, "you're a genius of sorts. What's your verdict on the other fellow?"

"Shoot him in the back," el Léon advised. "Throw heem in the *rio*. North of here, I theenk." Then, obviously to explain the reason for this piece of advice, he went on to give a short account of what had happened at Convido the night before, ending: "Others lie dead in my country. Their story weel be passed by the *autoridad* to Austin. Eet weel fit — eet weel all fit. And *muy amigo*, Roderigo Alvarez, weel have been avenged."

"I killed Alvarez," Lawson said, still probing and recklessly speculative. "I shot the varmint. You say he was your friend, Garcia. Wouldn't you like to avenge him yourself? I've been told you're pretty fast with a gun. Do you fancy matching the speed of your pistol against mine? All you have to do is ask Silas to give me my gun back."

"No," Garcia said, smiling in a manner that warned he was following the American's mind at every twist and turn. "So — it was you who keeled Roderigo. I thought as much, and geev you no chance. Nor do I forgeev. Tonight I weel return. Then, if the honoured *senor* weel permeet it, I weel hang you myself."

"Good fellow!" Bolsover chortled, evidently relieved by what el Léon intended and no doubt delighted to accept what would be experienced help in a grim undertaking where he had none. "You'll be mighty welcome, mister — and I'll be looking out for you!"

"Weeth the wheesky?"

"Why, dammit, Alfredo, you'll be welcome to every bottle I've got!" Bolsover declared, plainly having forgotten that he owed no gratitude to this man who had in fact placed him in his present predicament. "I'll put 'em out on the table for you!"

"I theenk I like that," the giant Mexican simpered.

"If you two could only hear yourselves!" Lawson spat contemptuously. "Silas, I don't think you mean to kill Hugh Brakes just yet. He needs help, man. Aside from anything else, he's bleeding all over the floor. Knowing Tina as I do, *she* won't like that."

"Hold your g'damn row about knowing my wife!" Bolsover cautioned ferociously, essaying a backhander.

"A fact is what is," Lawson said, apparently the most regretful of men. "You cannot change any one of 'em, Silas. Shame, isn't it?"

"I'll pay you, Clem!"

"Maybe you owe me more than you know," Lawson goaded, tongue in cheek.

"Don't you push me too far!"

"How far would that be?"

Bolsover's dark face flared. He looked like a Fury springing straight from the tips of hellfire. Now he drew back the barrel of his gun to smash.

"*Senor!*" Garcia pleaded aggrievedly. "Patience, I beg of you. The night weel soon be here."

Bolsover regained control of himself in the nick of time. "He's a trial!" he muttered hoarsely.

"The other man does bleed," el Léon reminded, pointing at the red spots which already marred the polish on the floor.

Bolsover nodded, wrinkling his steep nostrils fastidiously as he glanced down. Then, stepping to the threshold of the room, he opened the door and thrust his head into the passage outside. "Tina!" he called.

His wife answered at once from the direction of the kitchen. "Yes?"

"Will you come through here, please?"

Quick footfalls told of the woman's approach. Then Bolsover stepped back — covering the prisoners every second of the time — and let her into the room. "You're good at bandaging up, honey," the rancher observed, nodding at Brakes. "Will you do what you can for him?"

"He's in desperate need of a doctor, Silas," Tina said directly. "Hugh could bleed to death."

"There's just you, honey," Bolsover informed her — "you and nobody else. Apparently Doc Silk has gone to his reward. Besides, if he still lived, I wouldn't want him out here. Not today."

Nodding, the woman made nothing out of that. She stepped right up to Hugh Brakes and examined his wound as nearly as she could. "It's nasty," she said. "I don't want to pull it about in here. Hugh is hurting enough."

"Reckon the bone's broken?" Lawson asked.

"There's no sign of fragmentation where the bullet came out," Tina answered, as matter-of-fact about it as if she examined injuries of the severity

159

every day. "That proves nothing, of course. We can only be thankful that the bullet went straight through. I don't think anybody could do more here than clean up the wound and bind it."

"Hear that, Hugh?" Lawson inquired.

"Comforting," Brakes responded faintly. "Thank you, Mrs Bolsover."

"I hope you'll be saying as much when I've done with you," Tina said a trifle grimly. "Where do you want to put them, Silas?"

Bolsover seemed taken aback by his wife's question, and Lawson wondered whether the directness of Tina's words had brought home to him still further the icy reality of what he was doing. Robbing others of their freedom was another serious offence in criminal law. It might be less than murder, yet it was enough to provoke sobering thought. Though always a hard-headed businessman, Bolsover had also been honest enough in the past, and each time he contemplated something greatly illegal now there must be a jolt.

"Er, in the cellar," Bolsover hurried, once over the check in his speech. "Yes, we'll put them in the cellar. You can bring the medical box down there."

"Very well, Silas," the woman said, turning away and leaving the room.

Lawson eyed the giant rancher again. Bolsover was frowning to himself. He seemed puzzled by his wife's mute acceptance of what was happening. Perhaps he had been expecting censure — and was worried as to what might lie behind its absence. Lawson was himself a little dismayed by Tina's lack of reaction so far. The girl had a good head on her shoulders and must be able to see that her husband was inviting catastrophe. He had hoped that she would impress it on the man. The Bolsovers had so much to lose if the folly of today were allowed to run its course. Whatever the magnitude of Silas Bolsover's crime in co-operating with the Mexican *bandidos* — a situation in which some form of coercion could

161

conceivably be playing a part — he had not yet killed anybody. Murder was the point of no return. Indeed, if at this stage he would only round on Alfredo Garcia — denounce the man in town perhaps — he could still avoid actually going to prison. True, Texas folk could be vindictive and there was always the risk that some local vigilante committee would call him to account on a moonless night, but any man who acted against his fellows inevitably risked reaping the whirlwind. Yet, as Lawson saw it, Bolsover still had the chance of redemption, and it should not be thrown away. Especially by his wife. But perhaps Tessa knew what she was doing. Lawson hoped so.

"What are you staring at?" Bolsover suddenly demanded, indicating the door.

Lawson held his ground and got a firmer grip on the sagging Brakes. "Do you want me to answer that?"

Bolsover's silence suggested that he did.

"I was wondering how a man who already has so much can risk it all for just a little more."

"Get out of here!" Bolsover ordered disdainfully, using the muzzle of his pistol to point to the right.

Lawson eased his charge out of the study and into the passage beyond. Turning right here, they shuffled off in the direction of the kitchen; but soon, towards the end of the corridor and on the left, they came to a door which was set flush with the wall. Bolsover halted them, then opened the door himself, revealing the top of a flight of steps that led down into a gloomy room at the bottom of the house. "Down!" the giant rancher ordered.

Lifting Brakes bodily now, Lawson manouvred his foreman onto the steps and held him erect and steady. After that, with a supreme effort from Brakes and a lot of strength from his helper, they made it down to the cellar floor, where Lawson saw — in the light from a narrow fanlight set in the further wall at ground level — some sacks of grain and potatoes, a deal of fruit laid out in store, and several pieces of old or broken furniture. Among the latter stood a couch of imitation leather that still looked good for a turn or two, and Lawson steered Brakes to it and laid him out upon it. "All the comforts of home, eh?" Bolsover jeered, gazing down into the cellar from the top of the steps. "Don't imagine you have any hope of escaping. The fan is built into brown mortar and far too narrow to let a man through. And the door up here is two inches thick and has an iron deadlock."

"You have us for now," Lawson conceded.

"I have you for keeps, Clem," Bolsover said confidently. "I'm going to take the key from my pocket and lock you in now. My wife will no doubt be down presently. I'll be behind her. Up here — with this gun. All right?"

Lawson nodded curtly, and Bolsover

closed the door above and turned the key.

Starting to walk, Lawson went three times round the cellar like a caged animal, then, satisfied that there was indeed no way out except through the door at the top of the steps, he returned to the couch on which Brakes lay. The foreman's face was ashen, and his chin had rolled across his chest. He had obviously fainted off. Lawson checked his employee's vital signs, but could do nothing helpful and, seeing a straight-backed chair behind the head of the couch, went and seated himself upon it. After that, folding his arms, he sat and looked upwards at the door through which he expected Tina Bolsover to shortly appear.

In fact a number of minutes went by before the key again turned in the lock and Tina entered. She poised for a moment on the top step of the stone stairway, a basin of steaming water in her hands and a towel draped over her left forearm. Silas Bolsover appeared at his wife's back. Under his left arm he carried a medical chest, while he threatened the cellar floor from his other wing with the gun that he had warned about. Slowly bending at the knees, he set the box down on the top step, then backed off a little into the passage behind him. "Don't think of trying to take my wife hostage," he warned. "Do that, Clem, and I'll put a bullet into Brakes immediately. You can't cover your own and your foreman's body with one female form."

"Silas," Lawson said, repaying the rancher's recent contempt with some of his own, "I hadn't even given it a thought." He smiled as Tina reached him from the foot of the steps. "Thank you, ma'am. Would you like me to fetch the box down."

"No, Clem," she replied, flashing him a warning look. "I'll do it myself."

"Whatever you say."

The woman set the basin of hot water down beside the couch, letting the towel slip from her arm and fall across the body of the unconscious Brakes. After that she climbed back up the steps and lifted the medical box, returning with it to the couch. Then, lifting the lid of the chest, she took out a pair of scissors and, gazing at Brakes's left shoulder, worked the blades thoughtfully. "He's fainted, hasn't he?"

Lawson nodded.

"I'm glad of that," Tina said frankly. "I hate giving pain, and this would hurt a conscious man no end. I'm going to cut all the cloth away from that wound and clean it out as thoroughly as I can. Hugh is a very healthy man, and his flesh ought to heal without any trouble. It's the amount of blood he's lost that is so worrying."

"You can only do the best you can for him, Tina," Lawson said, his eye faintly questioning as he added: "We're in a pickle."

"That you are," she agreed.

"Tina — "

"No!" she breathed, her upturned face momentarily fierce.

"What's that?" Silas Bolsover demanded from above. "Speak up, Clem! If you've anything to say, I'd like to hear every word of it."

Lawson sucked breath irritably. "Can't I even speak now?"

"Sure — so long as I can hear every word."

"May you rot in hell!"

"That wasn't very nice, Clem," Tina Bolsover said sternly, starting to cut away the clothing from around Hugh Brakes's wound.

"Neither is he."

"He's my husband, Clem."

"Then it's about time he started behaving like it," Lawson informed her. "All he's doing right now is pull you down into the mire with him. How much loyalty does that command?"

Tina raised the finger encircled by her wedding ring. "As much as that."

The gun above went off. Its bullet missed Lawson's right ear by a fraction of an inch. Then it flew around the angles of the cellar, howling miserably before it fell with a small thud amidst a spread of dehydrating apples.

"Careful, Silas!" Tina urged reproachfully.

"Your friend has got too much to say!" her husband retorted.

"You did say you wanted to hear every word," she reminded. "Who says he's a friend of mine anyway?"

"Damn the pair of you then!" Lawson snapped, rising from his seat in a huff.

There was a warning click as Bolsover thumbed back the hammer of his gun again, but Lawson ignored it. Turning away from his chair, he walked towards the front of the cellar and halted under the narrow fanlight, gazing up at it and wishing that he understood the female of the species better. He could grasp why a good wife would go down with a husband who was misguided or stupid, but Bolsover had plainly gone to the bad and wasn't worth any consideration from a decent spouse. He needed pulling up sharply. Nothing else would do. Drawing upon the significance which the incident beside the pond had apparently imparted, Lawson had supposed Tina fully aware of that — and even desirous of doing what she could about it — but he wasn't so sure now. That strange touch in her nature, mercurial and inconstant — which balanced out its forthrightness — seemed to have been at work. She could have changed her mind, lost her nerve, or simply felt despair and thrown in her lot on the wrong side — because it seemed all she had. It appeared anyhow that he could look for no assistance, physical or verbal, from her reversed state, and he felt even more sick inside when he viewed what could be his limited future.

Though the cellar was irradiated by mistrust and hatred, silence now grew within it. The only sounds present were those made by Tina as she cut and sponged while treating Brakes's injured shoulder. Lawson went on staring at the fanlight. He did not turn again until about a half an hour later, when he heard the woman put away her scissors and medical things, and rise with a faint rustle of clothing from the crouch into which she had settled. After that, without moving his position, he watched her carry the medical chest back up the steps to the passage, return for the now bloodied bowl of water, then leave the cellar altogether without so much as a backward glance. But that, of course, had to be part and parcel of it, and he realized that he had no right to expect much else. He and Tina had once had that big romance — and somehow, he guessed, he had been relying on their residual friendship — because the male mind worked like that. Hell-and-dammit! He should have known better! When a woman stopped loving, she effectively stopped everything. He had known that before, and was merely encountering the fact of it here. If blame had to be apportioned, the fault was down to him.

The cellar door banged shut, and again the key grated in the lock. Noticing that the now heavily bandaged Brakes had recovered consciousness and was staring up at the ceiling, he returned to the man's side and got ready to ask him how he felt. But just then he noticed that a finger which had used plenty of water had printed a single word large upon the dusty tiling of the floor in the shadow of the couch. LATER.

Relief lifted a corner of his growing hopelessness. The message could only be Tina's. Perhaps he had misjudged her after all.

8

ONCE he had established that Brakes was comfortable and no longer in great pain, Lawson tried to make conversation with the man. This mostly concerned the best ways of treating the personalities about whom their difficulties centred. But it was soon apparent that, regardless of the fearful cloud which hung over them, Brakes lacked the energy and interest to discuss things for long. So Lawson let the talk fizzle out and renewed his prowling, helping himself to an apple or two and setting himself little problems of memory and arithmetic to help pass the time, for this had a tendency to drag since it had been indicated that there would come an hour during the day when the chance to escape would probably be provided.

Yet despite the boredom, the uncertain

light of the cellar made it hard to keep track of the passing hours, and he could only make a rough guess that it was getting towards the middle of the afternoon when he heard noises issuing from the door above the steps which suggested that somebody was trying to unlock it rather hastily and meeting with little success. The noises persisted and, soon feeling driven to it by nervous strain, Lawson went bounding up the steps and put his mouth near the keyhole. "Is that you, Tina?" he asked tensely.

"Yes," answered the woman's slightly muffled voice.

"You alone?"

She uttered another affirmative, and the key went on grating and jamming in the lock, seemingly a poor fit.

"What's up with the key?"

"It isn't the right one."

"Where is the right one?"

"Silas has got it in his pocket," the woman replied. "He's gone on his rounds — out on the range. This is the time I've been waiting for."

"That key is useless!" Lawson protested. "It's going to get stuck. What'll you tell, Silas?"

"It has unlocked this door," Tina retorted angrily, muttering to herself after that and fighting anew to make the lock turn. "I made a mistake over the key when I went to unlock the cellar one day. This wrong one unlocked the door, and has done it since; but I have to get it exactly right. Don't press me."

Lawson could understand how she felt, and he said no more.

The woman's battle with the lock went on for another minute and, while he did not doubt that Tina knew what she was talking about, Lawson slowly resigned himself to her ultimate failure; but then there was a dull metallic click and the door swung open, Tina putting a pink and slightly perspiring face around it and beckoning hard. "Get Hugh Brakes!"

"He's none too sharp, girl."

"Clem," she said gravely, "it's now or never."

"Bless you!"

"You may do," Tina observed dryly. "I'm coming with you, boy. I think Silas has gone out of his mind. I've argued with him, I've pleaded with him — I've even offered to take the blame myself. He won't listen!"

"I did wonder if it could be something like that," Lawson admitted. "Afraid of him?"

"He'll kill me for this — if he gets the chance."

"He'll have to kill me first," Lawson said, looking back down the steps and seeing that Hugh Brakes — perhaps more aware than he had supposed — had just pushed himself erect off the couch on which he had been lying and was now shakily approaching the foot of the climb. "Hugh!"

"I can manage, boss," the foreman said. "You stay where you are."

"Let him help himself," Tina urged.

"The less we have to do for him, the better for all."

"I see that," Lawson confessed. "Where are the horses?"

"There are no horses," the woman said. "Your own mounts have been put into our stables. There's no chance we can saddle and ride, Clem. It would be far too risky. This has to be done stealthily and afoot." She tut-tutted. "Oh, don't look so down in the mouth, man! We're only a mile or so from your grass. If we leave the front of the house, follow a nearby landfold I know of towards the river, and then pursue the bank of the Rio Grande southwards, we'll be on Box L grass in half an hour. Once there — so long as we haven't shown ourselves to anybody who might chase us — we'll be safe, and it will then be up to you to make any plan you like to bring about my husband's downfall."

"You make it sound easy," Lawson said. "I guess there's no reason why it shouldn't be. Let's get on with it."

Brakes had just finished toiling up the steps and joined his boss at the top. Now Lawson indicated that the foreman should walk between Tina Bolsover and him. The woman had already left the cellar doorway. She was moving down the passage to their right, presumably into the front of the house.

The two men hurried after the woman. Lawson saw Brakes's knees give a slight wobble every other step, but in the main the foreman appeared to gain strength from the exercise. In a moment they reached the hall. This part of the house did not look much used, and Tina, who was already at the front door and waiting for them, opened up onto what was literally a field of grass. After peeping out quickly, she led the way into the immediate range, bending left, and presently they entered a landfold which sank to the depth of a dozen feet and followed its long curve in the direction of the river, emerging in the growth along the edge of the

Rio Grande about five minutes later.

Now, moving through cottonwoods, willow, brush and cacti — often tangled up into thickets amidst which mesquite flourished — they walked and shouldered southwards, the crouched Tina moving with a familiarity which left Lawson and Brakes trailing in her wake and finally, in the case of the latter, failing. Then, after a last stumble, Brakes crawled in beneath a mass of overhanging willow and, collapsing on his back, gasped out: "Leave me here, boss. All I'm doing is slow you and the lady up. You can come back for me later. For what damned use I am to anybody at this time!"

"All right," Lawson said heavily, for the need to do what his foreman wished made him feel as if he were denying his principles. "I guess you'll be safe enough here for the time being. Take it easy, eh?"

"I don't know what else," the foreman said, as Mrs Bolsover completed about twenty yards of backtracking and rejoined them. "Apologies, ma'am. This is where I stop for now. I'm plumb done in. The spirit's willing but the flesh is weak."

"That's okay, Hugh," Tina said kindly. "You're doing the sensible thing. There's no need to push yourself beyond what you know you can stand. Perhaps you'll feel better later on."

"Maybe," Brakes responded, closing his eyes.

"When you like, Tina," Lawson prompted.

On they went again, Lawson now more or less keeping up, and they were preparing to leave cover near the spot where the Box L grass drove its wedge towards the river, when the giant figure of Alfredo Garcia stepped out of the greenery before them and the man showed his teeth in a threatening leer, right hand brandishing a Colt 'Dragoon' that looked big even in his grasp. "*Alto!*" he ordered. "Ah, the poor husband of thees woman! Eet is as he feared. Betrayal — *tración negro!* As well I do not go back to *Mejico* but seet myself here all day."

"By God!" Lawson exclaimed; for this latest piece of bad luck was too much to swallow — and he could not control the impulse to react against it, doing an abrupt little dance as he kicked powerfully at the revolver that the Mexican was holding.

The rising toe caught the pistol in the trigger-guard, and the weapon was torn from Garcia's grasp and went flying into the nearby brush. Without further thought, Lawson tore into the giant. He rifled two savage punches into el Léon's solar plexus and then banged him twice on the jaw, using similar force. Garcia, caught off guard — and still looking flushed from the considerable amount of strong whisky that he had swallowed earlier in the day — staggered backwards, clutching at his midriff and spitting blood.

Then he recovered himself and, gravely affronted, launched himself at

Lawson with a roar that went well with his soubriquet. About as muscular a specimen of manhood as his generation could show, he seemed to imagine that he could overwhelm his smaller attacker by sheer size and strength, but Lawson dodged under the giant's reaching arms and slid out to the left, loosing a right that nailed el Léon's jaw from such an angle that it literally spun the Mexican about face.

Garcia presented his posterior. The target was too good to miss. Lawson hopped again and let fly with his boot a second time. This kick, too, was perfectly delivered. It sent el Léon toppling forward into a patch of prickly pear. The big man flattened the heart of the clumped cactuses, but picked up dozens of spines from the growth surrounding the main area of impact. He rose in a hurry, tearing at his flesh and cursing volubly — beaten as much by sheer discomfort as anything else — and, though his assailant was far from satisfied and would have liked to make a real job of it, Lawson seized Tina Bolsover by her left hand and towed her into a full run, only releasing her when he perceived the risk of pulling her over by going that mite too fast for her length of leg.

Open grass stretched before the runners.

Lawson saw the Box L home buildings low upon the land to the northwest and knew that he was on his own ranch. He threw back his head, tucked in his elbows, and picked up his knees, pelting for the distant ranch house with every particle of energy that he possessed. Now he heard el Léon bawling at the rear. Garcia was ordering a pursuit of the fugitives by his followers who had been unseen by Lawson just now and presumably hidden from landward by the thicker growth on the riverbank nearer to the water.

It wasn't long before Lawson heard men yelling in the mingled pleasure and urgency of the chase. He prayed that they would pursue on foot — but imagined that this would prove a vain prayer — and almost at once a drubbing of hooves and equine snorting confirmed that heaven wasn't listening and his prayer was in vain. But he raced onwards, shouting back encouragement to Tina over his left shoulder — and the pair of them went on covering lots of ground smoothly enough, though it was now a certainty that they would soon be overtaken. This tremendous effort had to be all for nothing — no better than a wild, despairing gesture!

Iron shoes knocked hard against the earth, and horses reeked in the stagnant heat of the lengthening day. Then the Mexicans were there, mounts lunging between Lawson and his female companion. Harsh yet musical voices chivvied them almost good-naturedly, and then the lariats started to fly. Lawson ducked and dodged, eluding a couple of flying nooses, but heard a sobbing cry from Tina Bolsover and looked back to see that a rope had claimed the woman and already jerked her off her feet.

Lawson turned back towards Tina. There was no self-sacrifice in this because he knew that escape was impossible and simply didn't want to see his companion needlessly hurt. So he lunged over to where she was being rolled and tumbled by her captor and, catching hold of the rope between her and rider holding it, first checked the woman's spinning motion and then lay back with all his strength and weight, jerking the lariat taut in the yard or two of it which extended between the horseman and him, and the Mexican lifted from his saddle like a plucked cork and fell to the grass, his impact a shuddersome one. Then Lawson swung back to the woman and loosened the imprisoning noose from around her body, throwing it over her head and then helping her up, but the shadows of men and horses closed upon them instantly and a pistol roared, the bullet all but parting

Lawson's hair and warning him that further resistance could prove fatal. "They've got us!" he gasped at Tina. "If we'd only been closer to my ranch house, that shot might have brought somebody galloping!"

He looked despairingly towards the still quite distant buildings, but there was no trace of movement anywhere near them. Then a Mexican, patched, pop-eyed, and unwashed — but obviously as dangerous as he was scruffy — sent his horse bumping against Lawson, staggering him, then waved his smoking revolver back towards the river. "*Vamos, gringo — vamos!*"

In no position to argue it, Lawson shrugged, sleeved off, and put in a few long strides to help him catch up with Tina, who was already retracing the route to the Rio Grande under pressure from another bandido. The walk was one of almost half a mile, since the runners had covered even more ground than Lawson had calculated before the Mexican horsemen had caught up with them, and he had ample opportunity to get his breath back and feel the full measure of his apprehension before they neared el Léon again and he saw that Alfredo Garcia was still nipping cactus spines out of his flesh.

Garcia's face came round. Mouth bleeding, cheeks inflamed, and eyes reddened, the giant's face was hatred incarnate and he was literally palpitating — beside himself with fury indeed — and he suddenly ran at Lawson and let go with an almighty roundhouse swing. Sensing that if the punch landed it would most likely kill him, Lawson swayed back in an effort to avoid it, but it nevertheless clipped the point of his jaw and, though his attempt at evasion had robbed it of much of its force, it still contained power enough to instantly put his light out, and he toppled sideways and crashed to the ground without having any true awareness of what had happened.

He was from time to time after that dimly conscious of being pulled and thrown about; and, when he fully regained his senses — it could have been well over an hour later according to the state of the light — he was not all that surprised to discover that he had been subjected to abuse of a peculiarly Mexican kind; for they had tied him belly-down on the back of a horse — with his nose almost buried in its backside — and they had returned him to the Bolsover ranch house, where the mount involved in his humiliation had been ground-tied near the open front door.

By turning his head to what extent he could, Lawson was able to look into the front of the house. He saw Silas Bolsover and Alfredo Garcia standing together in the hall. They had come to high words, and the rancher was shaking a fist; but el Léon appeared to suddenly tire of the quarrel and thumbed his nose contemptuously at Bolsover. Now he turned away from the cattleman and walked out of the house, moving straight to the horse that bore the flattened Lawson. Freeing the still weak and groggy captive, he set him on the ground and shook him violently, slapping his face several times after that with a hand that was first open and then reversed. Finally, he squared Lawson with the front door of Bolsover's dwelling and shoved the prisoner through it, following up with a powerful and well directed kick that more or less paid Lawson out for the one that had sent the Mexican tumbling into the patch of prickly pear.

Nor was the punishment over. It was the turn of the still enraged Bolsover to seize Lawson. With his fingers bruising into the tops of the almost fainting captive's arms, he ran him towards the mouth of the passage that led through to the rear of the dwelling, abruptly propelling him into it, and Lawson promptly spun out of line and struck the wall on his right, rebounding into a fall which brought him thudding to his hands and knees. "Blame me, would he!" Bolsover raged. "Ah, the Mexican scum!" Then he sprang at his scapegoat and picked him up anew, flinging him forward again, this time with the kind of precision that dropped Lawson right outside the cellar door in the wall on the left.

After that, as Lawson sought to regain the vertical — more by instinct than sense — the crippled giant opened the door of the basement room that was clearly to be the captive's prison again and pitched him through it, Lawson tumbling end-over-tip down the flight of stone steps beyond and coming to rest in a spread of limbs on the dusty floor below. There, close to unconsciousness again, he let go, relaxing his bruised joints and knotted muscles, and he kept his eyes shut for a minute — slowly becoming aware that he was not alone in the cellar and that somebody was bending over him.

Raising his eyelids, he saw Tina Bolsover crouching close to him. Her face was swollen and she had the beginnings of two black-eyes. The sight brought home to Lawson, as nothing else could have done, the sheer brutality of which his enemies were capable, and he levered himself into a sitting position and gasped: "I suppose you're a prisoner too?"

"That she is!" Silas Bolsover's voice snarled from behind him. "And it's not less than she deserves!"

Lawson craned round and up at the top of the steps where the crippled rancher stood. "This woman is your wife, Bolsover!" he reminded. "I wouldn't have blamed her had she shot you in your sleep — or poisoned you at breakfast! Don't talk to me about what folk deserve! There's no fate too bad for you!"

"Why the devil did you have to go away for all that time a few years ago?" Bolsover demanded bitterly.

"You took real good advantage of it!" Lawson accused in return. "Filching another man's woman is hardly an honourable action!"

"I was never your woman, Clem!" Tina Bolsover snapped. "That's man-talk — king stallion stuff! I was never anybody's woman but my own! You went away. Most of the time you hardly bothered to write. You took me for granted. I could see that no woman was ever going to matter much to you."

"You knew why I was up north for so long!" Lawson protested. "It was thanks to my Uncle Tom that I got a start in ranching. He was there when I needed him, and I had to be there when he needed me. The poor fellow was a long time dying, that's the fact of it. I thought I could trust you, Tina; I believed I could depend on you to understand and help. It shot the guts out of me when I came home and learned that you had hitched up with Silas Bolsover."

"Shot the guts out of you!" Tina jeered. "What do you want me to credit? There have been plenty of women since. You've gained something of a name for your goings on in that direction!"

"You bet!" Lawson fired back defiantly. "I wasn't going to live like a monk over you. This is a case of the kettle calling the saucepan black. You had a string of beaux before we met up. Men talk, Tina — or some of them do."

"My business, Clem!"

"Isn't that the easy way out!"

"All you ever cared about was that ranch of yours!"

"And Silas is so different?" Lawson bit. "That husband of yours is well known to be a warm man. Are you worth a million yet, Silas? Or are you still topping up? Maybe that's why you've been on the take from that Mexican hellion, Alfredo Garcia!"

"They were once pals of a kind," Tina put in scornfully.

"Pals!"

"Fellow thieves might be more accurate," the woman admitted. "How do you think Silas got *his* start? It wouldn't be untrue to say that his first herd was a stolen one."

"How's that for a wife's loyalty?" Bolsover asked in a genuinely pained voice. "What were you after, Tina, but the best return you could get on your charms? No need to spit at Lawson and me for our ambition. Case of birds of a feather, honey! You're like us, I reckon, and maybe you deserve us both."

"This won't do," Lawson said. "It isn't a perfect world we live in. It's a market place from one end to the other. In it we buy what we can afford, Silas, and sell for the best we can get. That goes for me, you, Tina, and everybody else. Of course Tina's no better than we are. We all have to take care of ourselves before we can do much for others. There's no shame in making the best we can of our lives. But there are rules, Silas. Tina keeps them, and so do I. That's the difference. We may be birds of a similar feather, but similar is like unto and not the same as."

"Spare me that kind of clever talk,

Lawson!" Bolsover sneered.

"Okay, then. By their deeds shall ye know them."

"Do you prefer that?"

"Holy smoke!"

"Holy Writ, Silas — and don't mock it. You're up to your neck in trouble!"

"I've been that before — and got out of it."

"It was never like this time."

"How the heck would you know?" Bolsover demanded. "What's so different about this time?"

"You've crossed up the person most important to your success, man!" Lawson responded. "You've crossed up your own wife, and she isn't going to forgive you. This way or that, you're done for — and you must know it. Your only chance is to stop it right here!"

"You're trying to kid me there's no way out."

"I want you to reflect on it, Silas," Lawson said gravely, "before it's too late."

"How thoughtful of you!"

"As we're going," Lawson said, "you've got to murder Tina — because there must be no tongue left to speak other than for you. Careful of that. The workers on this ranch may be ready to keep quiet about what they suspect now, but let anything happen to Tina and I'll wager it would be a different story. How much real investigation do you figure your life will stand?"

Bolsover gave a spiteful chuckle. "I'm not going to harm my wife, Lawson. But can I be responsible for what Tina may do to herself? Heavens alive, Clem! Everybody around here knows how much that girl was once in love with you! But they also know that she's now a married woman — old 'Clubfoot's' missus — and just the one to stick by her marriage vows. What, then, if her heart yearns back to the other man? Women have often cracked in such circumstances. There have been suicide pacts — even in Texas. I don't reckon people would find it impossible to swallow if you were found hanging side by side in your barn tomorrow morning."

"Having first been hanged here by you and that big Mexican?"

"That's what we know that others don't know," Bolsover agreed, jerking his pistol fast as Lawson showed signs of getting up and turning on him. "So, you see, I do have a way out, don't I?"

Lawson shook his head emphatically — but he rather thought the other might be right.

9

WITH the key turned on them, Lawson and Tina were left to sit looking at each other in the dulling glow from the fanlight. He said little to her, and she said less to him. Everything about the cellar seemed a little unreal. Shadows ran together and shapes threatened to dissolve. They might have been looking into another world, and Lawson feared that that could indeed be the case. In the spirit of optimism, it was easy to believe that some basic goodness always remained — and that the worse couldn't happen — but everything here was in deadly earnest and being forced on by a pair of merciless villains who lived only for their own advantage. This could well prove a condemned cell with a window on the fabled Hades.

It grew dark in the cellar. Now

Lawson and the woman sat in total silence. When a small sound did enter the hush, it lingered like a mocking intruder. The tension screwed into Lawson's temples and knotted up his stomach. He felt gooseflesh prickle and cold sweat run. He wanted to pace, but couldn't see to do that. A sense of doom was gathering in the darkness, and the atmosphere of approaching death became a chill presence. Lawson felt there ought to be something which Tina and he could do, and yet there was nothing. They were imprisoned about as surely as two people had ever been. The sheer fact of it filled him with a silent scream!

Suddenly footfalls grew dully audible in the passage above the cellar's front. They stopped outside the door of the basement room. Then the key grated and the lock turned. Lawson looked towards the top of the steps adjacent. Two lanterns dazzled there. Now the men holding the lights began descending, and the captives rose involuntarily from their seats to meet the pair. "Okay, you two," Silas Bolsover said coldly, "let's get this over with!"

"We should tie them," the also present Alfredo Garcia observed.

"I don't want them slowed up," Bolsover retorted. "We're a poor couple if we can't conduct a man and a woman to my barn without losing them."

"As you weesh," Garcia responded shortly.

"I'll go first," Bolsover said. "You bring them along behind me."

"So," the Mexican acknowledged, gesturing with his pistol for the prisoners to take up the position that Bolsover had ordered.

Lawson stepped in behind the clubfooted rancher, hearing Tina and el Léon move into place at his back, and then the little procession climbed the steps and left the cellar, making a right turn in the passage above and heading for the front door. Bolsover opened this with a twist of his hand that was at once quick and slightly furtive, and the four of them passed out into the blackness of a night that was just perceptibly paled by a glimmer from the rising moon. Now they made their way around the northern end of the house and crossed the yard that extended down the dwelling's rear, approaching the ranch buildings at the further side of the space and slanting finally towards the barn, which stood some bit apart from the others on the far right.

They entered the barn through the wicket set in one of the twin leaves of the building's greater door. Here the light of the lanterns once more assumed its full importance. His senses heightened by fear, Lawson picked up the sweet, earthy odour of the place and felt its dryness and lingering heat, conscious of sweat once more trickling coldly at his brow. Then, halting the party under a beam — which could plainly be reached with ease by climbing a stack of filled corn sacks — Bolsover looked up and, putting his gun away, said: "Let's get those two hanging, Garcia. I came in earlier and placed a couple of lariats handy."

"You weel tie their wrists," the Mexican said.

"Keep them covered then!" Bolsover responded, nodding; and he set his lantern down on the floor and produced some piggin strings from a trouser-pocket. "Watch Lawson now!"

Lawson was indeed ready to attempt something desperate. The situation seemed to be slipping away utterly beyond him. He realized that Bolsover's wicked but daring plan required an unpunctured body to be sure of success, but he also knew that he would be instantly struck or gunned down at the first sign of a false move. His death was a virtual certainty whatever he did and, against that, the chance of some dubious post mortem triumph seemed a trifle absurd just then. He must obey his instinct to live and keep hanging on. A miracle could still occur — no matter how improbable that might seem at this last minute.

Thus he stood mute and erect while the clubfooted rancher secured first his wrists and then Tina's. After that he watched while Bolsover found the lariats of which he had spoken, climbed the pile of corn sacks, and threw the nooses over the convenient beam, leaving the loops dangling at just the right height and the slack of the ropes hanging down to the floor. Then, grasping that they had reached the moment of truth — and that he had somehow failed Tina Bolsover and himself — Lawson began to kick out in a kind of token struggle, aiming for the lantern standing nearby in the hope of causing a fire; but Bolsover instantly dropped to his buttocks and slid down over the heaped sacks to the floor, grabbing him by the scruff of the neck and shaking him as a dog might shake a rat. Finally he shoved Lawson's neck into the noose that awaited him, seized the slack of the hang-rope, and jerked tight with all his strength, lifting his victim off the ground and holding him in suspension — but only for a moment or two; for just then there was a clattering of hooves out in the ranch yard and a man's voice shouted peremptorily: "Where are you, Bolsover?"

Bolsover let go of the rope that held Lawson aloft, and he seemed to have been struck rigid as he stood there listening.

"*Silencio!*" Garcia warned tautly.

"Bolsover," the voice outside went on — "you get out here right now!"

Coughing and choking to open up his throat again, and shaking his head to get the ringing out of his ears, Lawson concentrated anew as he crouched there with the hang-rope coiling loosely about him. He recognised that voice. It belonged to Jack Crisp, the Box L's *segundo* and Hugh Brakes's great friend, the guy indeed who had been nominated to step into Brakes's' shoes when he took over the managership of the Lawson ranch and the master himself went off to war.

"Bolsover!"

"*Silencio!*" Garcia repeated sibilantly.

Out in the yard Jack Crisp changed his cry. "Mr Lawson? You around, boss?"

Lawson could see that the wicket was set ajar. If he obeyed el Léon and kept still and silent, all would still be lost for Tina and himself. It was necessary that he act before Crisp went away — escape from the barn if he could, then let matters sort themselves out as they would. There would no doubt be some risk to Tina, but she would also be defended by surprise; and, short of their captors shooting her down in cold blood — which he couldn't see happening at this time — he might soon be in the position to undertake her rescue himself. Yes, he judged the risks here worth taking — both for her and himself.

Thanking God that his legs were

still free, Lawson literally erupted into action. He plunged headlong at the wicket, and went through it with a crash — bullets ripping at the woodwork all around him — and he hit the earth outside and rolled, yelling, as he caught both his movement and his breath: "Jack — here!"

Sensing movement behind him, Lawson craned quickly over his left shoulder. He glimpsed the shape of Alfredo Garcia bending through the wicket. Fire streaked redly from the muzzle of the Mexican's pistol. Lead stirred the dust beside Lawson's left hand. He rolled again, wheeling forward on his right shoulder, and bullets chased him, each one only just missing some part of his body. Tasting dirt, he feared that each shot presaged his end, but the threatening weapon soon fell silent and he saw that riders were now galloping over to him from the middle of the yard. "There's not much forecast in this!" he announced sententiously, scrambling to his feet as a horseman reined in beside him.

"That you, boss?"

"Yes, it's me, Jack," Lawson answered. "They were holding me prisoner in there."

"Who's they?"

"Silas Bolsover and Alfredo Garcia. You know, el Léon."

"That great show-off!"

"They've got Tina Bolsover too."

"Yeah," Crisp mused, "Hugh said Bolsover's missus had got herself tangled up in this."

"Brakes?"

"He came staggering into the bunk-house an hour or so back," the *segundo* explained. "He told us where he'd been with you and what had happened. He said you ought to have reached home hours ago, and that you must have been caught again and brought back here. That's how come we showed up like this."

"And men were never more welcome," Lawson assured him, "or came more surely in the nick of time. What about Hugh? How's he now?"

"Looking pale about the gills," Crisp answered, "but I guess he'll be all right. Mrs Dupont has put him to bed in the house. She'll look after him like a son. She's got a soft spot for old Hugh."

"There are two or three worse men," Lawson acknowledged dryly. "So he dragged himself home. That was brave. What a relief for all concerned, by heck! So you know what Bolsover's been up to then?"

"We ought to string him up as a warning to any others like him!" Crisp declared. "Even our skunks and rattlers don't throw in with the greasers! No wonder those oily varmints have been able to come and go so easily around here!"

"He deserves a necktie party all right," Lawson agreed, reversing himself and offering his tied hands. "Cut me free, please."

Crisp took out a shut-knife; then, opening it, reached down and sliced through the thong that bound his employer's wrists.

"Thanks," Lawson said, massaging the spots where the piggin string had previously restricted his circulation and looking towards the black and soaring front of Bolsover's barn. "I've got to go back in there, Jack. I'd be obliged for the use of your pistol."

The *segundo* handed over his Colt. "You're going back into the barn?"

"Where else?"

"I've got a score of the boys here."

"Look after them — and yourself," Lawson ordered, since he could see a lot of movement — dim and uncertain — up the yard and outside the now fully illuminated 'Rocking Chair' bunkhouse. "We could find ourselves at odds with the Bolsover crew before this lot is over."

"Purely a social call!" Crisp protested. "We just rode over to fetch our boss."

"You make that plain to those men up the yard," Lawson advised. "Now keep back."

"If you say so," Crisp returned — "but I go to hell if I like it!"

Advancing on the wicket in the barn's front, Lawson thumbed back the hammer of his Colt. He could see that the two lanterns were still burning behind the small entrance to the building. He sensed no menacing movements within. These facts did not seem to add up in any way that he had expected. Good sense dictated that Bolsover and Garcia ought to have put out the lights before now. With the interior of the barn illuminated, they would be at a disadvantage under any form of attack, but would be in the reverse situation if they stood in the dark and fired at incoming shapes silhouetted against what light there was outside the wicket. Even so, it occurred to Lawson that he had been all indignation and brave talk up to now, for he had no clear idea of how he was going to tackle this. A direct advance on that little opening and the flimsy planking which surrounded it would amount to suicide. "Do you hear me in there?" he inquired tentatively, halting several yards short of the wicket. "We're in numbers out here. If you've got any sense, you'll step into the yard with your hands up!"

"Clem?" Tina Bolsover's voice called.

"You can hear it is."

"They've gone, Clem. I'm alone in here."

"Gone?" Lawson asked sharply. "How so?"

"There's a door at the back of this place."

Lawson pulled a wry jib to himself. A back door, eh? But of course there would be one. A building of the barn's size would have more than one entrance to it. He wasn't thinking too clearly right now. What with all this activity and being knocked unconscious to boot, it had been a very exhausting day. In fact Garcia and Bolsover had demonstrated the best kind of intelligence. Perceiving that events had tipped against them, they had done a bunk while the opportunity was there. Well, he'd go after them in due course. But first he must see Tina safe. Crisp and his men could take her home with them. She could wait for him there. He hoped they'd have a chance to talk before long — though he was by no means certain what they would talk about. He was only sure that, if she were taken to the Box L, she would at least still be around to derive whatever advantage might be present in the new situation that would inevitably materialise later on. "Come on out!" he urged. "It's safe enough out here, Tina. Just my boys. You may be able to talk to your own hands. I think they're a bit troubled as to what's going on."

The woman emerged from the barn. Her hands were still tied behind her back. Lawson freed them before leading her up the yard to where Jack Crisp was now explaining the apparent invasion of the 'Rocking Chair', by the Box L riders, to the Bolsover crew. The little *segundo's* tones were strained and defensive — since his explanations seemed to be incensing the 'Rocking Chair' employees rather than otherwise — and Lawson was afraid that real trouble might manifest if he didn't step in quickly. "This is Clem Lawson of the Box L!" he called, adding a friendly and calming note to the natural authority in his voice. "Sorry about this, you 'Rocking Chair' men, but we've got a bit of trouble. Your boss has been misbehaving. Like as not you fellows have a pretty good idea of what I'm talking about. Silas Bolsover has been assisting the Mexican, Alfredo Garcia, and his *bandidos* by allowing them to use the ford up river of here to drive stolen cattle over into Mexico. I've been trying to put a stop to it, and ended up Bolsover's prisoner on that account. But I'm free now, and believe that everything is in hand. I think Mrs Bolsover will be pleased to explain how matters stand, if you're still in any doubt, and I guess she'll answer any questions you may have too. After that you can all go back to bed or whatever you were doing before this incident occurred."

"It's Bill Grantly, ma'am, your foreman!" a deep voice called. "Say the word, and we'll put this pack of hounds off your land neck-and-crop!"

"Forget it, Bill!" Tina Bolsover advised. "Clem Lawson has just told you the truth. And my husband has run away to prove it. If you want to please me, take the men back indoors. I don't want anybody here to get hurt on Silas's account. He isn't worth it!"

"Very well, ma'am," Bill Grantly's voice returned obediently. "Just as long as we're not obeying Clem Lawson."

"You're doing what I asked," the woman assured him. "What you heard from Mr Lawson was simply good advice."

"Back indoors, men," Grantly ordered, his tall black shape turning into the cluster of muttering figures astir behind him. Then there was a slow surge back into the 'Rocking Chair' bunkhouse as the risen moon cast white light into the ranch yard down the ragged edge of a cloud that was tracing the nearby river westwards.

Suddenly a rifle cracked at the back of the space to the south of the barn. Uttering a brief gasp, Tina Bolsover crumpled to the ground. Lawson bent quickly towards the woman, as a second long gun spoke, and a bullet flew only inches above the top of his head. Turning away from the fallen Tina now — in the knowledge that he too was a selected target — he dived into the wide opening to the south of him, shaping to approach the unseen marksmen down this quarter of the ranch yard at a crouched run. The light improved still more, and his eyes focused. Ahead of him he made out the shapes of a number of horses and their riders. Then the two rifles flashed again, and the slugs barely missed him, one on either hand. He received the impression of two very large men, afoot and standing beside their horses, aiming at him again. In his right hand, Lawson still held Jack Crisp's revolver cocked and ready. Lifting his arm, he snapped off a quick one at the figure opposite the muzzle of his gun, and the other jerked backwards and cast his rifle from him, clutching at his chest as he steadied up and then doubling forward. Lawson was confident that he had just severely wounded Silas Bolsover, and he pulled up and set himself to finish the job, but the big rancher made a sudden grab for his reins and turned his mount across Lawson's sights, swinging up an instant later and swaying ominously in the saddle as he set off westwards.

The second rifle, unquestionably el Léon's, went off about then, but the shot missed by a yard — which suggested that the giant Mexican had been shaken — and he too mounted up and galloped off westwards, his followers spurring into motion likewise and forming up around him as a shield that Lawson did not attempt to penetrate with a further shot. Instead, swinging on his heel, he ran back to where Tina Bolsover lay and saw that Jack Crisp had dismounted and was crouching beside her. "How is it, Jack?" he inquired anxiously.

"Don't look good, boss," Crisp said, his small face blurring into a pale travesty of its normal faintly canine self as it turned up and round. "She's alive — but only just. Shot clear through the body."

"While there's life — "

"Well, yes, sir."

Crisp clearly considered the woman to be as good as dead. It was a terrific blow; perhaps the worst that Lawson had ever received. He stood there for an instant, fighting off the dark emotion that threatened to smother him, but he assimilated it all, fearing that some day he might be called on to pay dearly for his act of inner strength; and he went to the *segundo's* horse and said: "I'm taking your nag, Jacko. I've got something to do, and it won't wait."

"Kind of figured it might be like

that," Crisp said soberly.

Lawson stepped into the *segundo's* saddle. "Ask help of her own people," he ordered. "There's no doctor within an easy ride, so you'll have to do what you can for her." Then he rode out in front of his own cowboys and shouted: "Follow me, men, and ride hard! We're going to cut those Mexicans off before they cross the Rio Grande and wipe them out!"

Spurs raking, Lawson led off around the northern end of Bolsover's ranch house.

10

NOW Lawson gave thought only to what he must do. He virtually ignored all things about him in the moonlit night that did not contribute to his ends. His eyes were fixed upon the leading edge of the strip of dark cloud which still followed the river westwards. It formed a pointer of sorts, and he believed that it presently indicated the ford on the Rio Grande that he wished to reach in the shortest time possible. For he had worked out that, even if his party had been late in getting started, they were crossing unobstructed ground which was almost completely level and that that in itself must give them a real advantage over the men riding much closer to the river, who had brush to avoid in places and several irregularities in the formation of the bank itself which required care to negotiate. He feared that he might have been a little optimistic in stating to his followers that they were going to cut off the Mexican bandits and annihilate them — short of their re-entering Mexico he had meant — but he felt there could still be enough in their favour to make this extreme effort worthwhile.

In fact he realized, as his party neared the crossing, that the headlong rush would have achieved nothing if all had gone normally for both sides — since the Mexicans would have been over the river a minute or two ahead of his arrival — but, from what Lawson could make out as he glimpsed the bandits halted on the land just short of the ford, their leader had done something that he never would have expected and stopped to help Silas Bolsover, who appeared to have fallen off his horse and had to be picked up and put back in the saddle again. Whatever the exact details of this pause, the result was that Lawson's vision of overhauling the *bandidos* short of their re-entering Mexico had now been achieved, for the men across the way were never going to get moving again before the pursuers got within range of them.

In truth, the Mexicans were so taken up with the Bolsover problem that they did not seem to grasp the danger they were in until the very last moment. Then one of their number twigged the body of horsemen dashing at them from the north and called out to the rest. El Léon, guiding the horse bearing Bolsover's hunched shape, shouted frantically for resumed flight and headed for the ford, adding a demand for cover. The company of *bandidos* first pressed in behind the leading pair and then halted on the bank above the edge of the crossing and turned to face the oncoming riders with guns blazing.

The charging cowboys instantly returned fire. Lawson aimed along the side of his mount's neck and added his blast to the general racket.

Behind him somewhere he heard a man cry out in pain, then saw a Mexican who sat directly before his eye fold up and pitch to the ground over the near-side shoulder of his horse. The exchange grew hotter by the moment and, at about twenty yards from the enemy, Lawson drew rein and was conscious of his followers doing the same. Effectively, lines of battle had been drawn and it was now simply a matter of shooting back and forth in a contest of nerve and attrition which was rendered the more frightening by the ashen moonglow. Gun muzzles seemed to spit out scarlet blossoms and the coughing of black powder just failed to cover the soft squeak and rattle of detachable cylinders making their rounds on worn spindles that had been used too often and oiled too little. Every facet of sight and sound seemed to exaggerate a hundredfold, and the excretions of horses and the sweat of human fear had the same bitter flavour as the burned explosives.

Men went on falling. It became evident that the fight was becoming one-sided. Mexican saddles were emptying so fast that the bandits who still lived were tending to sit petrified and wait for it, their now empty guns still upraised. When Lawson had spoken in terms of wiping the Mexicans out, he had been voicing his grief and anger as much as anything else — and had taken it for granted that all his enemies would not fall — but suddenly he perceived that here again his wish was being granted in total, for the *bandidos* were being gunned down to a man.

The battle ended quite abruptly. Lawson wasn't truly aware that it was all over until his recently deafened ears picked up the muttering of voices about him. The black shapes of the Mexicans now carpeted the ground, though the odd man stirred and a few groans were audible. He looked at the figures lying there, and wondered how many children had just been orphaned and wives widowed. But this was still no time for thoughts of that kind. Lawson realized that the men who lay there had really mattered very little to him. Silas Bolsover and Alfredo Garcia were his quarry, and he would know no rest until they were dead. The worst of it was that the two giants had escaped across the river and he would have to chase them in the country on the other side. Lawson had intended never to enter Mexico again illegally, but the events of the night were about to force him into a second crossing of the Rio Grande whether he liked it or not. And he had better get on with it.

"I want you men to clear up here!" he called to his employees. "Get the bodies into Blazeville, and any wounded to the 'Rocking Chair'! I'm going over the river on my own! I'll see to any bigger arrangements that have to be made when I get back!"

No voice was raised as he ceased speaking, and he didn't hang about to encourage thought.

Instead he spurred his borrowed

horse forward, skirting the shot figures on the bank ahead. Then he jumped his mount down to the shore and gazed across the broad waters beyond. After that he pushed on over the firm bottom under the silvery flow, slapping with a hand and using a word or two of command, and presently he reached the further shore again and peered into the black shadows at the mouth of the valley which carried the trail into Old Mexico.

Entering the dark ingress, Lawson tried to get into Alfredo Garcia's mind, reckoning that no genius was needed to do that. El Léon had a badly wounded man on his hands, and would feel his need for freedom the more because of it. He would obviously try to get Silas Bolsover to the doctor in Convido as quickly as he could. But the probability was that the two men were making fairly slow progress, and he felt that he should overtake them well short of their goal. He could not ignore the possibility, of course, that Garcia had received a prevision of what had occurred back at the ford, and that the man would divert, hide, or even set up a shooting position on spec, but Lawson could not really see it, and was content to keep forging ahead with an openness based on the belief that the huge Mexican would ignore all cautionary imaginings and hold back only if forced to do so.

All this was not to say that Lawson did not remain watchful. Much of the apprehension that he had felt when previously in this valley returned to him now — for the mind was like that — and he kept peering deeply into the ever-present shades of his confined route and listening with ears that strained far beyond the echoing clatter raised by his horse. While Convido or thereabouts was his expected goal, he was still prepared for anything.

And that was just as well. For, as the valley began to widen and some essence of Mexico beyond reared at him as an intangibly forbidding presence, he saw a horse standing in the middle of the way before him, and then, as moonlight eddied in a skein of drifting vapour, made out a figure leaning against a boulder that dwarfed even his huge presence. "Bolsover?" he asked tensely, reining back and suddenly conscious that he had put up an empty revolver before leaving the Texas side of the Rio Grande.

"He figured you might show up, Lawson," Bolsover responded. "It was tight back there."

"My men won, Silas. If Garcia survives this night, he'll have to start over."

"Has its points, you know."

"I suppose so. He leave you?"

"I told him to go on," Bolsover explained grimly. "I'm a dead man, Lawson, but I want company into hell."

"Where hatred has it all, eh?"

"Where I'll find that accursed wife of mine again."

"Maybe not."

"She's still alive?" Bolsover asked quickly, his voice holding a sour and disappointed note.

"She was when I left your ranch," Lawson answered, feeling the stock of Jack Crisp's Henry repeating rifle against his right knee. "A strong woman — our Tina."

"What was that?"

"You heard me, Silas."

"You taunting son-of-a!" Bolsover raged, fire streaking from his right fist.

Lawson felt the bullet pluck the back of his collar as the *segundo's* rifle came clear of its boot. Pumping the weapon's action, Lawson instinctively leaned away as Bolsover's second slug creased the top of Crisp's big Texas pommel and burned leather stank. Then, the pressures of haste actually causing his eyes to start, Lawson got his own first shot in — the Henry jumping in his grasp as the shell detonated under its hammer — and the bullet slammed

Bolsover hard against the rock at his back, the man's knees buckling slightly as he rebounded from the contact with his pistol still blazing. He hung there for a full second longer while Lawson put two more shots through his body; then down he went, sprawling onto his back, and the last of his life left him in a great shudder which caused his heels to drum.

Cocking the Henry rifle again, Lawson released a pent up breath but looked around him with the greatest uncertainty. He simply could not credit that el Léon had ridden tamely away. Alfredo Garcia was too much the known opportunist for that. On leaving Bolsover, he would have wanted to be sure whether anybody did indeed come chasing up from the direction of the river; then to see how the action involving Bolsover turned out; and it was all Eldorado's gold to a tin trouser-button that he was still watching right now and preparing to trigger the sneak shot which he hoped would end the Lawson menace once and for all.

Lawson sprang off his horse. At the instant his feet hit the ground, the anticipated bullet tore through his hair, burning his scalp just perceptibly but doing no real harm. Crouching, Lawson was conscious of the gunflash still burning brightly in the tail of his left eye and, zig zagging, he advanced on the position from which the shot had come, praying devoutly that Jack Crisp's rifle was no average cowboy's weapon and loaded with only two or three cartridges. In this light, it was impossible to gain any clue to the state of the Henry's magazine, and the rifle might already be empty for what he knew.

He could see a reef of stone ahead of him now. The formation was nigger-black and sharply serrated, and the glow of the moon hovered above it without coming near. Once more fire spat at Lawson and the echoes of the shot rent and rolled. Again missed by the breadth of a hair, the American felt his temper snap. "Face me like a man, you cowardly Mexican greaseball!" he yelled, spittle flying.

"I fear you not, *gringo!*" el Léon bawled in reply, and rose up, ogre-like, behind the reef, his own rifle coming into line at the level of his hip.

Lawson could hardly believe his luck, but he didn't question it and, finding his gun on target, squeezed off. Mercifully, his fear concerning the rifle's magazine was not realized, for an explosion answered his trigger and Alfredo Garcia toppled backwards, his own weapon flashing a yard high. Lawson heard the man come to rest in an unbroken fall, and was fairly sure that the one bullet had been enough. Nevertheless he moved with caution as he rounded the line of rock behind which the Mexican had tumbled; and, arriving beside the inert figure with a final spring, put the muzzle of his rifle to Garcia's left temple. Now he jabbed several times in a manner that would have been extremely painful to a living man; but the bandit chief did not stir, and the examination which Lawson then carried out showed all signs of life to be extinct. His bullet had pierced Garcia's heart. El Léon was no more — and Mexico, no less than Texas, was probably the safer for it.

Lawson left the body and returned to his horse. There he thrust Jack Crisp's repeating rifle back into its scabbard. After that he mounted up and, conscious of being very much alone in the night, fetched round and began riding back towards the river. He felt tired — badly drained — far too spent, indeed, to give even a thought to picking up the two dead giants and laying them in earth. Tomorrow and the men of the morrow must take care of the remains. And if the coyote or the buzzard should obtain a sly feed — Well, bird and beast had to live, and Bolsover and Garcia would be feeding flesh of a like kind.

Coming to the Rio Grande, Lawson

let his horse cross it at a slow, splashing walk. The wind blew softly, and a distorted moon shone up at him out of the rippling flow. He could smell the prairie ahead and the trampled flowers of the season. The scents brought funereal visions to his mind. He knew that he had just done a considerable job for Texas, yet couldn't feel happy about it, for behind everything else lay the war. It was all part of the absurd upside down state of things. When men got noble and started fighting for causes, the world began to fall apart. Folk regularly gave in to temptations which they would ordinarily have ignored. Thus with Silas Bolsover and his petty greed. Even el Léon had been a victim of sorts. The present weakness of the law on the Texas side of the river had given him delusions of grandeur. A few years ago he had known his place and gone robbing in Coahuila for pesos. If the great brute had not been so vile, his posturing would have been funny.

The horse bore Lawson clear of the river. Then it crossed the shore and lifted over the bank beyond, giving a little snort of pleasure as it trotted towards a rider who had just halted a much bigger mount a short distance ahead. Ah, Jack Crisp. Lawson raised a perfunctory hand in salute. This would have to do with Tina Bolsover. Lawson took a deep breath and steeled himself to meet what he feared must come. "Hello, Jack."

"Hi, Mr Lawson. Kinda liberated your horse from the 'Rocking Chair' stables."

"I see that."

"Want to switch?"

"No hurry. This mustang of yours does very well."

"She's a dolly," Crisp approved.

"Well, Jack?"

"She died about an hour ago, sir," the *segundo* said heavily. "She didn't come round or anything. I rode out here in the hope of meeting you. I figured you'd rather hear it like this."

"Yes. Thank you."

"Her husband?"

"Dead — and Alfredo Garcia too."

"That's that then."

Lawson nodded. Done was done. It hurt about Tina. She had died despite him, and a man never quite got over a woman like that. Yet it was probably for the best. Too much had been said; too much light had played on the seamier side of human nature; and too much truth had become evident. Ignorance was indeed bliss, and only a fool sought to be wise.

"There's a rumour going about, boss," Crisp remarked.

"What's that, Jack?"

"That Mayor Wilberforce has appointed you the law."

"That's right," Lawson said deliberately, for he knew that he could not go back on the things that he had already done. "I'm the District Marshal."

You could blame that on the war as well.

Other titles in the
Linford Western Library:

TOP HAND
Wade Everett

The Broken T was big. But no ranch is big enough to let a man hide from himself.

GUN WOLVES OF LOBO BASIN
Lee Floren

The Feud was a blood debt. When Smoke Talbot found the outlaws who gunned down his folks he aimed to nail their hide to the barn door.

SHOTGUN SHARKEY
Marshall Grover

The westbound coach carrying the indomitable Larry and Stretch headed for a shooting showdown.

FIGHTING RAMROD
Charles N. Heckelmann

Most men would have cut their losses, but Frazer counted the bullets in his guns and said he'd soak the range in blood before he'd give up another inch of what was his.

LONE GUN
Eric Allen

Smoke Blackbird had been away too long. The Lequires had seized the Blackbird farm, forcing the Indians and settlers off, and no one seemed willing to fight! He had to fight alone.

THE THIRD RIDER
Barry Cord

Mel Rawlins wasn't going to let anything stand in his way. His father was murdered, his two brothers gone. Now Mel rode for vengeance.

ARIZONA DRIFTERS
W. C. Tuttle

When drifting Dutton and Lonnie Steelman decide to become partners they find that they have a common enemy in the formidable Thurston brothers.

TOMBSTONE
Matt Braun

Wells Fargo paid Luke Starbuck to outgun the silver-thieving stagecoach gang at Tombstone. Before long Luke can see the only thing bearing fruit in this eldorado will be the gallows tree.

HIGH BORDER RIDERS
Lee Floren

Buckshot McKee and Tortilla Joe cut the trail of a border tough who was running Mexican beef into Texas. They stopped the smuggler in his tracks.

BRETT RANDALL, GAMBLER
E. B. Mann

Larry Day had the choice of running away from the law or of assuming a dead man's place. No matter what he decided he was bound to end up dead.

THE GUNSHARP
William R. Cox

The Eggerleys weren't very smart. They trained their sights on Will Carney and Arizona's biggest blood bath began.

THE DEPUTY OF SAN RIANO
Lawrence A. Keating and
Al. P. Nelson

When a man fell dead from his horse, Ed Grant was spotted riding away from the scene. The deputy sheriff rode out after him and came up against everything from gunfire to dynamite.

FARGO: MASSACRE RIVER
John Benteen

The ambushers up ahead had now blocked the road. Fargo's convoy was a jumble, a perfect target for the insurgents' weapons!

SUNDANCE: DEATH IN THE LAVA
John Benteen

The Modoc's captured the wagon train and its cargo of gold. But now the halfbreed they called Sundance was going after it . . .

HARSH RECKONING
Phil Ketchum

Five years of keeping himself alive in a brutal prison had made Brand tough and careless about who he gunned down . . .

FARGO: PANAMA GOLD
John Benteen

With foreign money behind him, Buckner was going to destroy the Panama Canal before it could be completed. Fargo's job was to stop Buckner.

FARGO: THE SHARPSHOOTERS
John Benteen

The Canfield clan, thirty strong were raising hell in Texas. Fargo was tough enough to hold his own against the whole clan.

PISTOL LAW
Paul Evan Lehman

Lance Jones came back to Mustang for just one thing — revenge! Revenge on the people who had him thrown in jail.

HELL RIDERS
Steve Mensing

Wade Walker's kid brother, Duane, was locked up in the Silver City jail facing a rope at dawn. Wade was a ruthless outlaw, but he was smart, and he had vowed to have his brother out of jail before morning!

DESERT OF THE DAMNED
Nelson Nye

The law was after him for the murder of a marshal — a murder he didn't commit. Breen was after him for revenge — and Breen wouldn't stop at anything . . . blackmail, a frameup . . . or murder.

DAY OF THE COMANCHEROS
Steven C. Lawrence

Their very name struck terror into men's hearts — the Comancheros, a savage army of cutthroats who swept across Texas, leaving behind a bloodstained trail of robbery and murder.

SUNDANCE: SILENT ENEMY
John Benteen

A lone crazed Cheyenne was on a personal war path. They needed to pit one man against one crazed Indian. That man was Sundance.

LASSITER
Jack Slade

Lassiter wasn't the kind of man to listen to reason. Cross him once and he'll hold a grudge for years to come — if he let you live that long.

LAST STAGE TO GOMORRAH
Barry Cord

Jeff Carter, tough ex-riverboat gambler, now had himself a horse ranch that kept him free from gunfights and card games. Until Sturvesant of Wells Fargo showed up.

McALLISTER
ON THE
COMANCHE CROSSING
Matt Chisholm

The Comanche, McAllister owes
them a life — and the trail is soaked
with the blood of the men who had
tried to outrun them before.

QUICK-TRIGGER COUNTRY
Clem Colt

Turkey Red hooked up with Curly
Bill Graham's outlaw crew. But
wholesale murder was out of Turk's
line, so when range war flared he
bucked the whole border gang
alone . . .

CAMPAIGNING
Jim Miller

Ambushed on the Santa Fe trail,
Sean Callahan is saved by two
Indian strangers. But there'll be
more lead and arrows flying before
the band join Kit Carson against the
Comanches.

GUNSLINGER'S RANGE
Jackson Cole

Three escaped convicts are out for revenge. They won't rest until they put a bullet through the head of the dirty snake who locked them behind bars.

RUSTLER'S TRAIL
Lee Floren

Jim Carlin knew he would have to stand up and fight because he had staked his claim right in the middle of Big Ike Outland's best grass.

THE TRUTH ABOUT SNAKE RIDGE
Marshall Grover

The troubleshooters came to San Cristobal to help the needy. For Larry and Stretch the turmoil began with a brawl and then an ambush.

WOLF DOG RANGE
Lee Floren

Will Ardery would stop at nothing, unless something stopped him first — like a bullet from Pete Manly's gun.

DEVIL'S DINERO
Marshall Grover

Plagued by remorse, a rich old reprobate hired the Texas Troubleshooters to deliver a fortune in greenbacks to each of his victims.

GUNS OF FURY
Ernest Haycox

Dane Starr, alias Dan Smith, wanted to close the door on his past and hang up his guns, but people wouldn't let him.

DONOVAN
Elmer Kelton

Donovan was supposed to be dead. Uncle Joe Vickers had fired off both barrels of a shotgun into the vicious outlaw's face as he was escaping from jail. Now Uncle Joe had been shot — in just the same way.

CODE OF THE GUN
Gordon D. Shirreffs

MacLean came riding home, with saddle tramp written all over him, but sewn in his shirt-lining was an Arizona Ranger's star.

GAMBLER'S GUN LUCK
Brett Austen

Gamblers seldom live long. Parker was a hell of a gambler. It was his life — or his death . . .

ORPHAN'S PREFERRED
Jim Miller

Sean Callahan answers the call of the Pony Express and fights Indians and outlaws to get the mail through.

DAY OF THE BUZZARD
T. V. Olsen

All Val Penmark cared about was getting the men who killed his wife.

THE MANHUNTER
Gordon D. Shirreffs

Lee Kershaw knew that every Rurale in the territory was on the lookout for him. But the offer of $5,000 in gold to find five small pieces of leather was too good to turn down.

RIDE A LONE TRAIL
Gordon D. Shirreffs

The valley was about to explode into open range war. All it needed was the fuse and Ken Macklin was it.

HARD MAN WITH A GUN
Charles N. Heckelmann

After Bob Keegan lost the girl he loved and the ranch he had sweated blood to build, he had nothing left but his guts and his guns but he figured that was enough.

SUNDANCE: IRON MEN
Peter McCurtin

Sundance, assigned to save the railroad from a murder spree, soon came to realise that he'd have to fight fire with fire, bullets with bullets and death with death!

RIFLES ON THE RANGE
Lee Floren

Doc Mike and the farmer stood there alone between Smith and Watson. There was this moment of stillness, and then the roar would start. And somebody would die . . .

HARTIGAN
Marshall Grover

Hartigan had come to Cornerstone to die. He chose the time and the place, and Main Street became a battlefield.

SUNDANCE: OVERKILL
John Benteen

When a wealthy banker's daughter was kidnapped by the Cheyenne, he offered Sundance $10,000 to rescue the girl.